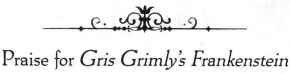

Praise for *Gris Grimly's Frankenstein*

"Grimly's fans have been awaiting this reworking of Shelley's 1818 classic for four years, and they will rejoice in the end result. Readers encountering the story for the first time may find Grimly's images rise to view whenever they think of it."

—*Publishers Weekly* (starred review)

"Grimly proves himself a more adept assembler of parts than his subject proved to be; his product is no monster, but a pastiche of style and substance that will reanimate the original for yet another generation of readers."

—*BCCB* (starred review)

"From the neo-Victorian clothing and emo hairdos to the steampunk backdrop of Victor Frankenstein's lab, Grimly's unique and twisted style blends perfectly with the material and breathes new life into these characters and situations.... Grimly's beautiful and trim version is a great way to immerse a new audience in this important work."

—*SLJ*

"Grimly's haunting illustrations dramatically show the range of human emotion connected with Frankenstein and his monster—rage, despair, hurt, lament, and even joy and excitement. Though often dark, Grimly's version has a whimsical quality that will draw teens in and allow them to better access this classic novel."

—*VOYA*

"Gris has a natural empathy with the disfranchised, the lost. It is very telling that he, like me, is attracted to Frankenstein and Pinocchio—lost souls abandoned by their creators in an uncaring universe. His line work becomes more elegant and precise with each book but it also becomes more and more emotional and expressive. Gris is a fabulist with the soul of a graveyard poet."

—Guillermo del Toro, director of *Hellboy* and *Pan's Labyrinth*

Naomi Ellis

Gris Grimly's
FRANKENSTEIN

OR

The Modern Prometheus

ASSEMBLED FROM THE ORIGINAL TEXT

BY

MARY SHELLEY

IN THREE VOLUMES

NEW YORK
PRINTED FOR BALZER + BRAY
HarperCollins Publishers
MMXIII

Balzer + Bray is an imprint of HarperCollins Publishers.

Gris Grimly's Frankenstein
Illustrations and afterword copyright © 2013 by Gris Grimly
Foreword copyright © 2013 by Bernie Wrightson
All rights reserved. Manufactured in the U.S.A.

www.epicreads.com

Library of Congress Cataloging-in-Publication Data
Grimly, Gris.
 Gris Grimly's Frankenstein, or, The modern Prometheus / assembled from the original text by Mary Shelley in three volumes. — 1st ed.
  p.   cm.
 Summary: Retells, in graphic novel format, Mary Shelley's classic tale of a monster, assembled by a scientist from parts of dead bodies, who develops a mind of his own as he learns to loathe himself and hate his creator.
 ISBN 978-0-06-186297-7 (trade bdg.) — ISBN 978-0-06-186298-4 (pbk.)
 1. Graphic novels. [1. Graphic novels. 2. Monsters—Fiction. 3. Horror stories.] I. Shelley, Mary Wollstonecraft, 1797–1851. Frankenstein. II. Title. III. Title: Frankenstein. IV. Title: Modern Prometheus.
PZ7.7.G76Gri 2013   2010046237
741.5'973—dc22   CIP
[Fic]   AC

Typography by Dana Fritts
21 22 WOR 12
❖
First Edition
Text originally published in 1818

For my parents, Lyle and Karen,
who never abandoned me

—G.G.

DID I REQUEST THEE,
MAKER, FROM MY CLAY

TO MOULD ME MAN?
DID I SOLICIT THEE

FROM DARKNESS TO
PROMOTE ME?

—PARADISE LOST

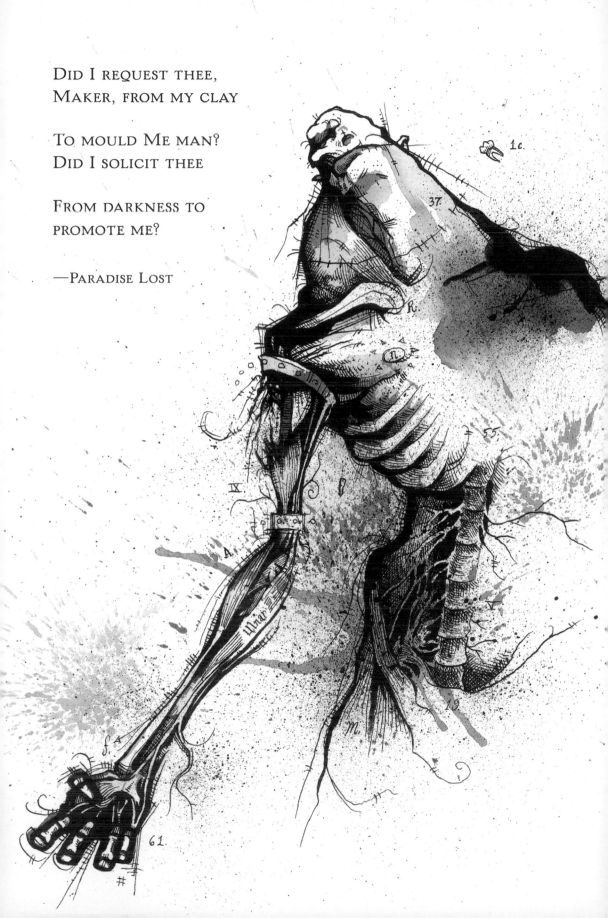

TABLE OF CONTENTS

FOREWORD

by

BERNIE WRIGHTSON

I was twelve or thirteen before I got all the way through *Frankenstein*. I had tried to read it twice already, and failed both times. My mental image was of rolling up my sleeves and going at it with a pick and shovel. Hard work.

Frankenstein is not an easy read. The language is extravagant and convoluted, and my expectations, like almost everyone else's, I suppose, had been formed by the movies. It is a book of ideas, not melodrama (despite its many melodramatic moments), quite unlike the comic books and Edgar Rice Burroughs novels I was used to. Still, after reading it, I realized I had unearthed a treasure.

I illustrated the story more than thirty years ago. Just my own visual interpretation, one more in the long line of interpretations—on stage, on film, and in print—since the book's original publication in 1818. No big deal. I wanted to do my version of it only because I loved the story. Nothing more than that. Since then I've been told by many people that it was my pictures that drew them into the book, that got them to read it cover to cover, and that they wouldn't have been able to read it at all had it not been for my illustrations pulling them along. I realized that I had done something much more than just decorate a favorite story: I had created a gateway into the book for the reader. Like a carnival barker whose spiel pulls the crowds into the sideshow tent, I had actually pulled them into the book and then carried them through the story. This, to me, was a big deal! A big responsibility. If I'd thought of that at the time, I probably would've been too intimidated to illustrate it in the first place.

When Gris told me he was planning to illustrate *Frankenstein,* I was delighted. Also a little nervous. I didn't say it, but I thought, Jeez, I hope he knows what he's getting into. I hope he realizes what a responsibility this is. I needn't have worried. Gris gets it.

I've known Gris ten or fifteen years now, and I've been a fan of his work from the start. Whether it's a single drawing or a series of drawings in a storybook, he's always brought a delightfully twisted sensibility to his work, a wonderful sly stylization—and always with a twinkle in his artist's eye. His work communicates. It pulls you in. It carries you along.

Here, in *Frankenstein,* from the first page, he takes you by the hand and pulls you into the story, seeming to say, again with that twinkle in his eye, "C'mon along. Don't be afraid. You'll love this." Gris Grimly, like all the great illustrators, knows his responsibility. He stands at the gateway, the key that unlocks the heart of the story in his hand, ready to help you unearth the treasure that lies within.

November 2012

VOLUME

I

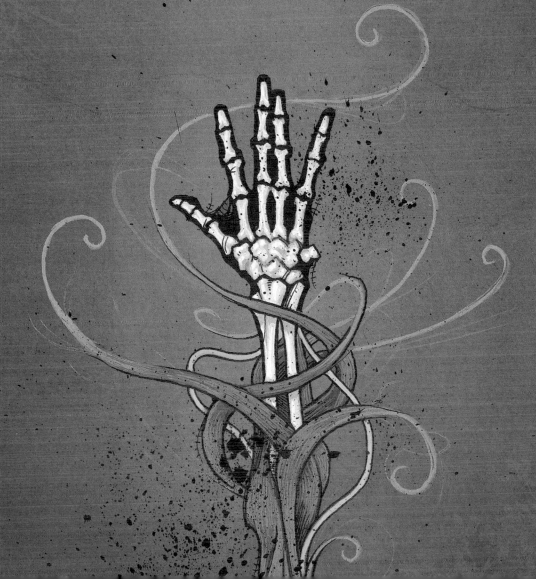

To Mrs. Saville, England.
—St. Petersburgh, Dec. 11th

You will rejoice to hear that no disaster has accompanied the commencement of an enterprise which you have regarded with such evil forebodings. I arrived here yesterday, and my first task is to assure my dear sister of my welfare, and increasing confidence in the success of my undertaking.

I am already far north of London; and as I walk in the streets of Petersburgh, I feel a cold northern breeze play upon my cheeks, which braces my nerves, and fills me with delight. Do you understand this feeling? This breeze, which has travelled from the regions towards which I am advancing, gives me a foretaste of those icy climes. Inspirited by this wind of promise, my daydreams become more fervent and vivid. I try in vain to be persuaded that the pole is the seat of frost and desolation; it ever presents itself to my imagination as the region of beauty and delight. There, Margaret, the sun is for ever visible, its broad disk just skirting the horizon, and diffusing a perpetual splendour. What may not be expected in a country of eternal light? I may there discover the wondrous power which attracts the needle; and may regulate a thousand celestial observations, that require only this voyage to render their seeming eccentricities consistent for ever. I shall satiate my ardent curiosity with the sight of a part of the world never before visited, and may tread a land never before imprinted by the foot of man. These are my enticements, and they are sufficient to conquer all fear of danger or death, and to induce me to commence this laborious voyage. But, supposing all these conjectures to be false, you cannot contest the inestimable benefit which I shall confer on all mankind to the last generation, by discovering a passage near the pole to those countries, to reach which at present so many months are requisite; or by ascertaining the secret of the magnet, which, if at all possible, can only be effected by an undertaking such as mines.

These reflections have dispelled the agitation with which I began my letter; and I feel my heart glow with an enthusiasm which elevates me to heaven; for nothing contributes so much to tranquillize the mind as a steady purpose—a point on which the soul may fix its intellectual eye. This expedition has been the favourite dream of my early years. You may remember, that a history of all the voyages made for purposes of discovery composed the whole of our good Uncle Thomas's library. My education was neglected, yet I was passionately fond of reading. These volumes were my study day and night.

My life might have been passed in ease and luxury, but I preferred glory to every enticement that wealth placed in my path. My courage and my resolution is firm; but my hopes fluctuate, and my spirits are often depressed. I am about to proceed on a long and difficult voyage; the emergencies of which will demand all my fortitude: I am required not only to raise the spirits of others, but sometimes to sustain my own, when theirs are failing.

I shall depart in a fortnight or three weeks; and my intention is to hire a ship, which can easily be done by paying the insurance for the owner, and to engage as many sailors as I think necessary among those who are accustomed to the whale-fishing. I do not intend to sail until the month of June: and when shall I return? Ah, dear sister, how can I answer this question? If I succeed, many, many months, perhaps years, will pass before you and I may meet. If I fail, you will see me again soon, or never.

Farewell, my dear, excellent Margaret. Heaven shower down blessings on you, and save me, that I may again and again testify my gratitude for all your love and kindness.

Your affectionate brother,

R. Walton

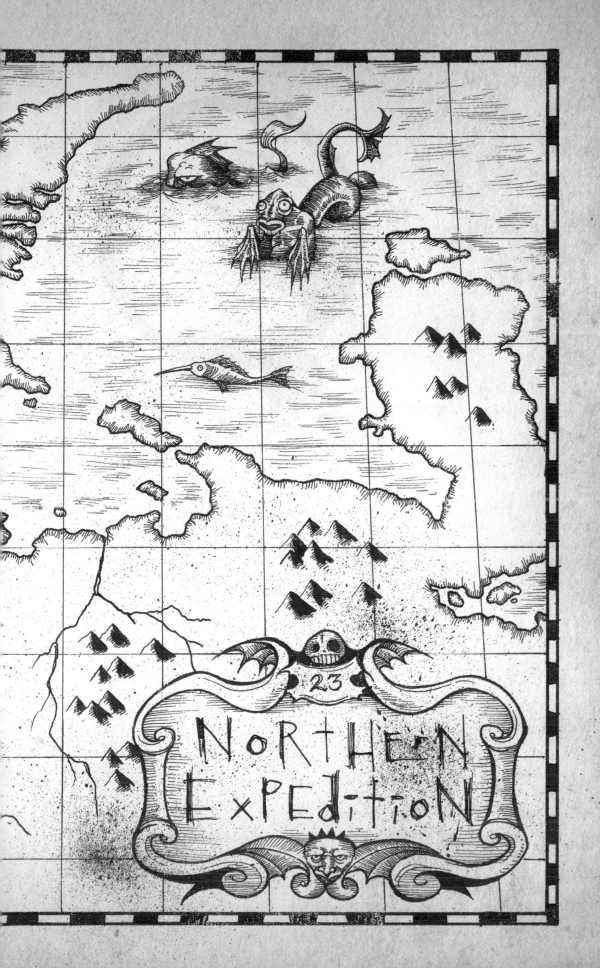

23

NORTHEN
EXPEDiTiON

To Mrs. Saville, England.
Archangel, 28th March

How slowly the time passes here, encompassed as I am by frost and snow; yet a second step is taken towards my enterprise. I have hired a vessel, and am occupied in collecting my sailors; those whom I have already engaged appear to be men on whom I can depend, and are certainly possessed of dauntless courage.

But I have one want which I have never yet been able to satisfy. I have no friend, Margaret: when I am glowing with the enthusiasm of success, there will be none to participate my joy; if I am assailed by disappointment, no one will endeavour to sustain me in dejection. I shall commit my thoughts to paper, it is true; but that is a poor medium for the communication of feeling. I have no one near me, gentle yet courageous, possessed of a cultivated as well as of a capacious mind, whose tastes are like my own, to approve or amend my plans. I am twenty-eight, and am in reality more illiterate than many school-boys of fifteen. It is true that I have thought more, and that my daydreams are more extended and magnificent; but they want keeping; and I greatly need a friend who would have sense enough not to despise me as romantic, and affection enough for me to endeavour to regulate my mind.

Well, these are useless complaints; I shall certainly find no friend on the wide ocean, nor even here in Archangel, among merchants and seamen. Yet some feelings, unallied to the dross of human nature, beat even in these rugged bosoms. My lieutenant, for instance, is a man of wonderful courage and enterprise; he is madly desirous of glory. He is an Englishman, and, in the midst of national and professional prejudices, unsoftened by cultivation, retains some of the noblest endowments of humanity.

The master is a person of an excellent disposition, and is remarkable in the ship for his gentleness, and the mildness of his discipline. He is, indeed, of so amiable a nature, that he will not hunt (a favourite, and almost the only amusement here), because he cannot endure to spill blood. He is, moreover, heroically generous. Some years ago he loved a young Russian lady, of moderate fortune; and having amassed a considerable sum in prize-money, the father of the girl consented to the match. He saw his mistress once before the destined ceremony; but she was bathed in tears, and throwing herself at his feet, entreated him to spare her, confessing at the same time that she loved another, but that he was poor, and that her father would never consent to the union. My generous friend reassured the suppliant, and, on being informed of the name of her lover, instantly abandoned his pursuit.

But do not suppose that, because I complain a little, or because I can conceive a consolation for my toils which I may never know, that I am wavering in my resolutions. Those are as fixed as fate, and my voyage is only now delayed until the weather shall permit my embarkation. The winter has been dreadfully severe; but the spring promises well.

I cannot describe to you my sensations on the near prospect of my undertaking. It is impossible to communicate to you a conception of the trembling sensation, half pleasurable and half fearful, with which I am preparing to depart. I am going to unexplored regions, to "the land of mist and snow;" but I shall kill no albatross, therefore do not be alarmed for my safety.

Continue to write to me by every opportunity: I may receive your letters (though the chance is very doubtful) on some occasions when I need them most to support my spirits. I love you very tenderly. Remember me with affection, should you never hear from me again.

Your affectionate brother,

R. Walton

To Mrs. Saville, England
July 7th

My dear Sister,

I write a few lines in haste, to say that I am safe, and well advanced on my voyage. This letter will reach England by a merchant-man now on its homeward voyage from Archangel; more fortunate than I, who may not see my native land, perhaps, for many years. I am, however, in good spirits: my men are bold, and apparently firm of purpose; nor do the floating sheets of ice that continually pass us, indicating the dangers of the region towards which we are advancing, appear to dismay them. We have already reached a very high latitude; but it is the height of summer, and although not so warm as in England, the southern gales, which blow us speedily towards those shores which I so ardently desire to attain, breathe a degree of renovating warmth which I had not expected.

No incidents have hitherto befallen us that would make a figure in a letter. One or two stiff gales, and the breaking of a mast, are accidents which experienced navigators scarcely remember to record; and I shall be well content, if nothing worse happen to us during our voyage.

Adieu, my dear Margaret. Be assured, that for my own sake, as well as yours, I will not rashly encounter danger. I will be cool, persevering, and prudent.

Most affectionately yours,

R. W.

To Mrs. Saville, England
August 5th

Do strange an accident has happened to us, that I cannot forbear recording it, although it is very probable that you will see me before these papers can come into your possession.

Last Monday (July 31st) we were nearly surrounded by ice, which closed in the ship on all sides, scarcely leaving her the sea room in which she floated. Our situation was somewhat dangerous, especially as we were compassed round by a very thick fog. We accordingly lay to, hoping that some change would take place in the atmosphere and weather.

About two o'clock the mist cleared away, and we beheld, stretched out in every direction, vast and irregular plains of ice, which seemed to have no end. Some of my comrades groaned, and my own mind began to grow watchful with anxious thoughts, when a strange sight suddenly attracted our attention. We perceived a low carriage, fixed on a sledge and drawn by dogs, pass on towards the north, at the distance of half a mile: a being which had the shape of a man, but apparently of gigantic stature, sat in the sledge, and guided the dogs. We watched the rapid progress of the traveller with our telescopes, until he was lost among the distant inequalities of the ice.

We were, as we believed, many hundred miles from any land; but this apparition seemed to denote that it was not, in reality, so distant as we had supposed. Shut in, however, by ice, it was impossible to follow his track.

About two hours after this occurrence, we heard the ground sea, and before night the ice broke, and freed our ship. We, however, lay to until the morning, fearing to encounter in the dark those large loose masses which float about after the breaking up of the ice. I profited of this time to rest for a few hours.

In the morning, however, as soon as it was light, I went upon deck, and found all the sailors busy on one side of the vessel, apparently talking to some one in the sea. It was, in fact, a sledge, like that we had seen before, which had drifted towards us in the night, on a large fragment of ice. Only one dog remained alive; but there was a human being within it, whom the sailors were persuading to enter the vessel. He was not, as the other traveller seemed to be, a savage inhabitant of some undiscovered island, but an European. When I appeared on deck, the master said, "Here is our captain, and he will not allow you to perish on the open sea."

On perceiving me, the stranger addressed me in English, although with a foreign accent. "Before I come on board your vessel," said he, "will you have the kindness to inform me whither you are bound?"

You may conceive my astonishment on hearing such a question addressed to me from a man on the brink of destruction. I replied, however, that we were on a voyage of discovery towards the northern pole.

Upon hearing this he appeared satisfied, and consented to come on board. His limbs were nearly frozen, and his body dreadfully emaciated by fatigue and suffering. I never saw a man in so wretched a condition. We attempted to carry him into the cabin; but as soon as he had quitted the fresh air, he fainted. We accordingly brought him back to the deck, and restored him to animation by rubbing him with brandy, and forcing him to swallow a small quantity. As soon as he shewed signs of life, we wrapped him up in blankets, and placed him near the chimney of the kitchen-stove. By slow degrees he recovered, and ate a little soup.

Two days passed in this manner before he was able to speak; and I often feared that his sufferings had deprived him of understanding. When he had in some measure recovered, I removed him to my own cabin, and attended on him as much as my duty would permit. I never saw a more interesting creature: his eyes have generally an expression of wildness, and even madness; but there are moments when his whole countenance is lighted up with a beam of benevolence and sweetness that I never saw equalled. But he is generally melancholy and despairing; and sometimes he gnashes his teeth, as if impatient of the weight of woes that oppresses him.

When my guest was a little recovered, I had great trouble to keep off the men, who wished to ask him a thousand questions; but I would not allow him to be tormented by their idle curiosity.

Once, however, the lieutenant asked, Why he had come so far upon the ice in so strange a vehicle?

His countenance instantly assumed an aspect of the deepest gloom, and he replied, "To seek one who fled from me."

"And did the man whom you pursued travel in the same fashion?"

"Yes."

"Then I fancy we have seen him; for the day before we picked you up, we saw some dogs drawing a sledge, with a man in it, across the ice."

This aroused the stranger's attention; and he asked a multitude of questions concerning the route which the demon, as he called him, had pursued, and if I thought that the breaking up of the ice had destroyed the other sledge. I replied, that I could not answer with any degree of certainty; for the ice had not broken until near midnight, and the traveller might have arrived at a place of safety before that time; but of this I could not judge.

From this time the stranger seemed very eager to be upon deck, to watch for the sledge which had before appeared; but I have persuaded him to remain in the cabin, for he is far too weak to sustain the rawness of the atmosphere. But I have promised that some one should watch for him, and give him instant notice if any new object should appear in sight.

Such is my journal of what relates to this strange occurrence up to the present day. The stranger has gradually improved in health, but is very silent, and appears uneasy when anyone except myself enters his cabin. For my own part, I begin to love him as a brother; and his constant and deep grief fills me with sympathy and compassion. He must have been a noble creature in his better days, being even now in wreck so attractive and amiable.

I said in one of my letters, my dear Margaret, that I should find no friend on the wide ocean; yet I have found a man who, before his spirit had been broken by misery, I should have been happy to have possessed as the brother of my heart.

I shall continue my journal concerning the stranger at intervals, should I have any fresh incidents to record.

August 13th

My affection for my guest increases every day. He excites at once my admiration and my pity to an astonishing degree. He is so gentle, yet so wise; his mind is so cultivated; and when he speaks, although his words are culled with the choicest art, yet they flow with rapidity and unparalleled eloquence.

He is now much recovered from his illness, and is continually on the deck, apparently watching for the sledge that preceded his own. He has asked me many questions concerning my design; and I have related my little history frankly to him. He appeared pleased with the confidence, and suggested several alterations in my plan, which I shall find exceedingly useful. He is often overcome by gloom, and then he sits by himself, and tries to overcome all that is sullen or unsocial in his humour. These paroxysms pass from him like a cloud from before the sun, though his dejection never leaves him. I have endeavoured to win his confidence; and I trust that I have succeeded. One day I mentioned to him the desire I had always felt of finding a friend who might sympathize with me, and direct me by his counsel.

"I agree with you," replied the stranger; "in believing that friendship is not only a desirable, but a possible acquisition. I once had a friend, the most noble of human creatures, and am entitled, therefore, to judge respecting friendship. You have hope, and the world before you, and have no cause for despair. But I— I have lost every thing, and cannot begin life anew."

As he said this, his countenance became expressive of a calm settled grief that touched me to the heart. But he was silent, and presently retired to his cabin.

August 19th

---Yesterday the stranger said to me, "You may easily perceive, Captain Walton, that I have suffered great and unparalleled misfortunes. I had determined, once, that the memory of these evils should die with me; but you have won me to alter my determination. You seek for knowledge and wisdom, as I once did; and I ardently hope that the gratification of your wishes may not be a serpent to sting you, as mine has been. I do not know that the relation of my misfortunes will be useful to you; yet, if you are inclined, listen to my tale. I believe that the strange incidents connected with it will afford a view of nature, which may enlarge your faculties and understanding. You will hear of powers and occurrences, such as you have been accustomed to believe impossible: but I do not doubt that my tale conveys in its series internal evidence of the truth of the events of which it is composed."

You may easily imagine that I was much gratified by the offered communication, yet I could not endure that he should renew his grief by a recital of his misfortunes. I felt the greatest eagerness to hear the promised narrative, partly from curiosity, and partly from a strong desire to ameliorate his fate, if it were in my power. I expressed these feelings in my answer.

"I thank you," he replied, "for your sympathy, but it is useless; my fate is nearly fulfilled. I wait but for one event, and then I shall repose in peace. Nothing can alter my destiny; listen to my history, and you will perceive how irrevocably it is determined."

He then told me, that he would commence his narrative the next day when I should be at leisure. I have resolved every night, when I am not engaged, to record, as nearly as possible in his own words, what he has related during the day. This manuscript will doubtless afford you the greatest pleasure: but to me, who know him, and who hear it from his own lips, with what interest and sympathy shall I read it in some future day!

R. Walton

I am by birth a Genevese; and my family is one of the most distinguished of that republic. My ancestors had been for many years counsellors and syndics; and my father had filled several public situations with honour and reputation. He was respected by all who knew him for his integrity and indefatigable attention to public business.

One of his most intimate friends was a merchant, who, from a flourishing state, fell into poverty. This man, whose name was Beaufort, was of a proud and unbending disposition, and could not bear to live in poverty and oblivion in the same country where he had formerly been distinguished for his rank and magnificence. Having paid his debts, therefore, in the most honourable manner, he retreated with his daughter to the town of Lucerne, where he lived unknown and in wretchedness.

My father loved Beaufort with the truest friendship, and resolved to seek him out and endeavour to persuade him to begin the world again through his credit and assistance.

Beaufort lay on a bed of sickness, incapable of any exertion. His daughter attended him with the greatest tenderness. Several months passed in this manner. Her father grew worse, and in the tenth month died in her arms, leaving her an orphan and a beggar. This last blow overcame her; and she knelt by Beaufort's coffin, weeping bitterly, when my father entered the chamber. He came like a protecting spirit to the poor girl, and after the interment of his friend he conducted her to Geneva. Two years after this event Caroline became his wife.

When my father became a husband and a parent, he found his time so occupied by the duties of his new situation, that he relinquished many of his public employments, and devoted himself to the education of his children. Of these I was the eldest, and the destined successor to all his labours and utility. But before I continue my narrative, I must record an incident which took place when I was four years of age.

My father had a sister, whom he tenderly loved, and who had married early in life an Italian gentleman. Soon after her marriage, she had accompanied her husband into his native country, and for some years my father had very little communication with her. About the time I mentioned she died; and a few months afterwards he received a letter from her husband requesting my father to take charge of the infant Elizabeth, the only child of his deceased sister.

I have often heard my mother say that she was at that time the most beautiful child she had ever seen, and shewed signs even then of a gentle and affectionate disposition. These indications, and a desire to bind as closely as possible the ties of domestic love, determined my mother to consider Elizabeth as my future wife.

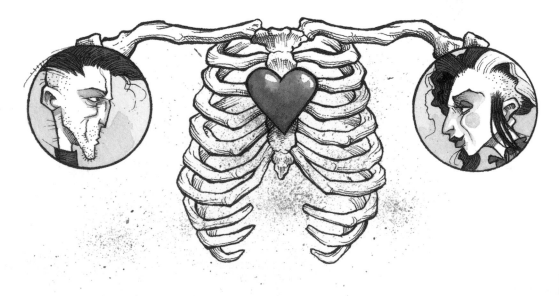

From this time Elizabeth Lavenza became my playfellow, and, as we grew older, my friend. Although there was a great dissimilitude in our characters, there was an harmony in that very dissimilitude. I delighted in investigating the facts relative to the actual world; she busied herself in following the aërial creations of the poets. The world was to me a secret, which I desired to discover; to her it was a vacancy, which she sought to people with imaginations of her own.

My brothers were considerably younger than myself; but I had a friend in one of my schoolfellows, who compensated for this deficiency. Henry Clerval was a boy of singular talent and fancy.

I remember, when he was nine years old, he wrote a fairy tale, which was the delight and amazement of all his companions. His favourite study consisted in books of chivalry and romance; and when very young, I can remember, that we used to act plays composed by him out of these favourite books.

I feel pleasure in dwelling on the recollections of childhood, before misfortune had tainted my mind, and changed its bright visions of extensive usefulness into gloomy and narrow reflections upon self. But, in drawing the picture of my early days, I must not omit to record those events which led, by insensible steps to my after tale of misery.

When I was thirteen years of age, I chanced to find a volume of the works of Cornelius Agrippa. I opened it with apathy; the theory which he attempts to demonstrate, and the wonderful facts which he relates, soon changed this feeling into enthusiasm. A new light seemed to dawn upon my mind; and, bounding with joy, I communicated my discovery to my father.

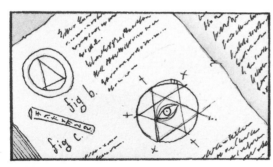

"Ah! Cornelius Agrippa! My dear Victor, do not waste your time upon this; it is sad trash."

If, instead of this remark, my father had taken the pains to explain to me that the principles of Agrippa had been entirely exploded, and that a modern system of science had been introduced, I should certainly have thrown Agrippa aside, but the cursory glance my father had taken of my volume by no means assured me that he was acquainted with its contents; and I continued to read with the greatest avidity.

My first care was to procure the whole works of this author, and afterwards of Paracelsus and Albertus Magnus. I read and studied the wild fancies of these writers with delight; they appeared to me treasures known to few beside myself.

It may appear very strange, that a disciple of Albertus Magnus should arise in the eighteenth century; but our family was not scientifical, and I had not attended any of the lectures given at the schools of Geneva. My dreams were therefore undisturbed by reality; and I entered with the greatest diligence into the search of the philosopher's stone and the elixir of life. But the latter obtained my undivided attention: wealth was an inferior object; but what glory would attend the discovery, if I could banish disease from the human frame, and render man invulnerable to any but a violent death!

Nor were these my only visions. The raising of ghosts or devils was a promise liberally accorded by my favourite authors, the fulfilment of which I most eagerly sought; and if my incantations were always unsuccessful, I attributed the failure rather to my own inexperience and mistake, than to a want of skill or fidelity in my instructors.

When I was about fifteen years old, we witnessed a most violent and terrible thunderstorm. It advanced from behind the mountains of Jura; and the thunder burst at once with frightful loudness from various quarters of the heavens. I remained, while the storm lasted, watching its progress with curiosity and delight. As I stood at the door, on a sudden I beheld a stream of fire issue from an old and beautiful oak, which stood about twenty yards from our house; and so soon as the dazzling light vanished, the oak had disappeared, and nothing remained but a blasted stump. I never beheld anything so utterly destroyed.

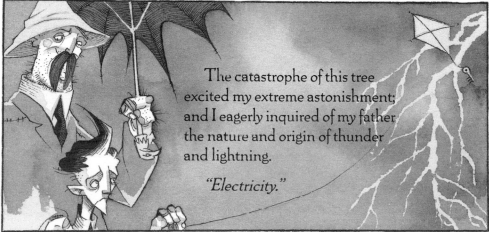

The catastrophe of this tree excited my extreme astonishment; and I eagerly inquired of my father the nature and origin of thunder and lightning.

"Electricity."

Another task also devolved upon me, when I became the instructor of my brothers. Ernest was six years younger than myself, and was my principal pupil. He had been afflicted with ill health from his infancy, through which Elizabeth and I had been his constant nurses: his disposition was gentle, but he was incapable of any severe application.

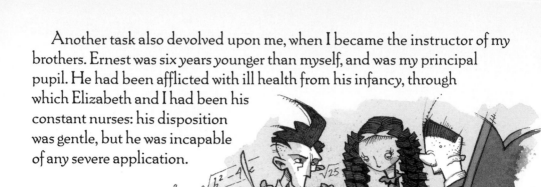

William, the youngest of our family, was yet an infant, and the most beautiful little fellow in the world; his lively blue eyes, dimpled cheeks, and endearing manners, inspired the tenderest affection.

Such was our domestic circle, from which care and pain seemed for ever banished. My father directed our studies, and my mother partook of our enjoyments.

CHAPTER TWO

When I had attained the age of seventeen, my parents resolved that I should become a student at the university of Ingolstadt. My departure was therefore fixed at an early date; but, before the day resolved upon could arrive, the first misfortune of my life occurred—an omen, as it were, of my future misery.

Elizabeth had caught the scarlet fever; but her illness was not severe, and she quickly recovered. During her confinement, many arguments had been urged to persuade my mother to refrain from attending upon her. She had, at first, yielded to our entreaties; but when she heard that her favourite was recovering, she could no longer debar herself, and entered her chamber long before the danger of infection was past.

The consequences of this imprudence were fatal. On the third day my mother sickened; her fever was very malignant, and the looks of her attendants prognosticated the worst event.

"My children, my firmest hopes of future happiness were placed on the prospect of your union. Elizabeth, my love, you must supply my place to your younger cousins.

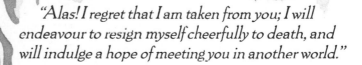

"Alas! I regret that I am taken from you; I will endeavour to resign myself cheerfully to death, and will indulge a hope of meeting you in another world."

She died calmly; and
her countenance expressed
affection even in death.
I need not describe the
feelings of those whose
dearest ties are rent by
that most irreparable evil,
the void that presents
itself to the soul, and the
despair that is exhibited
on the countenance. It is so
long before the mind can
persuade itself that she,
whom we saw every day,
and whose very existence
appeared a part of our own,
can have departed for ever.
The time at length arrives,
when grief is rather an
indulgence than a necessity.
My mother was dead, but
we had still duties which we
ought to perform; we must
continue our course with
the rest, and learn to think
ourselves fortunate, whilst
one remains whom the
spoiler has not seized.

My journey to Ingolstadt, which had been deferred by these events, was now again determined upon. This period was spent sadly; my mother's death, and my speedy departure, depressed our spirits; but Elizabeth endeavoured to renew the spirit of cheerfulness in our little society. I never beheld her so enchanting as at this time, when she was continually endeavouring to contribute to the happiness of others, entirely forgetful of herself.

The day of my departure at length arrived. I had taken leave of all my friends, excepting Clerval, who spent the last evening with us. He bitterly lamented that he was unable to accompany me: but his father could not be persuaded to part with him, intending that he should become a partner with him in business.

Tears gushed from the eyes of Elizabeth.

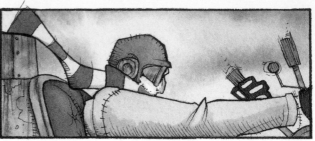

I threw myself into the chaise that was to convey me away, and indulged in the most melancholy reflections. I, who had ever been surrounded by amiable companions, was now alone.

I loved my brothers, Elizabeth, and Clerval; these were "old familiar faces;" but I believed myself totally unfitted for the company of strangers. Such were my reflections as I commenced my journey; but as I proceeded, my spirits and hopes rose. I ardently desired the acquisition of knowledge.

I had often, when at home, thought it hard to remain during my youth cooped up in one place, and had longed to enter the world, and take my station among other human beings. My journey to Ingolstadt was long and fatiguing. At length the high white steeple of the town met my eyes. I alighted, and was conducted to my solitary apartment, to spend the evening as I pleased.

The next morning I paid a visit to some of the principal professors, and among others to M. Krempe, professor of natural philosophy. I mentioned, it is true, with fear and trembling, the only authors I had ever read upon those subjects. The professor stared.

"Have you really spent your time in studying such nonsense?

"Every minute that you have wasted on those books is utterly and entirely lost.

"You have burdened your memory with exploded systems, and useless names. Good God! These fancies are a thousand years old, and as musty as they are ancient. I little expected in this enlightened and scientific age to find a disciple of Albertus Magnus and Paracelsus."

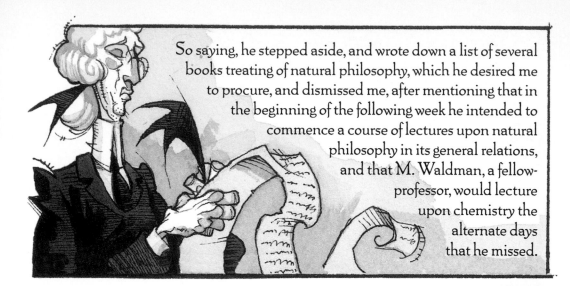

So saying, he stepped aside, and wrote down a list of several books treating of natural philosophy, which he desired me to procure, and dismissed me, after mentioning that in the beginning of the following week he intended to commence a course of lectures upon natural philosophy in its general relations, and that M. Waldman, a fellow-professor, would lecture upon chemistry the alternate days that he missed.

I returned home, not disappointed, for I had long considered those authors useless whom the professor had so strongly reprobated; but I did not feel much inclined to study the books which I had procured at his recommendation. I had a contempt for the uses of modern natural philosophy.

It was very different, when the masters of the science sought immortality and power; such views, although futile, were grand: but now the scene was changed. The ambition of the inquirer seemed to limit itself to the annihilation of those visions on which my interest in science was chiefly founded. I was required to exchange chimeras of boundless grandeur for realities of little worth.

My reflections during the first two or three days were spent almost in solitude.

Partly from curiosity, and partly from idleness, I went into the lecturing room. M. Waldman entered shortly after. This professor was very unlike his colleague. He began his lecture by a recapitulation of the history of chemistry.

"The ancient teachers of this science promised impossibilities, and performed nothing. The modern masters promise very little; but these philosophers have indeed performed miracles. They penetrate into the recesses of nature, and shew how she works in her hiding places. They ascend into the heavens; they have discovered how the blood circulates, and the nature of the air we breathe.

"They have acquired new and almost unlimited powers; they can command the thunders of heaven, mimic the earthquake, and even mock the invisible world with its own shadows."

I departed highly pleased with the professor, and paid him a visit the same evening. He heard my little narration concerning my studies, and smiled at the names of Cornelius Agrippa and Paracelsus, without the contempt that M. Krempe had exhibited. His lecture had removed my prejudices against modern chemists; and I requested his advice concerning the books I ought to procure.

"*I am happy to have gained a disciple; and if your application equals your ability, I have no doubt of your success. Chemistry is that branch of natural philosophy in which the greatest improvements have been and may be made. If your wish is to become really a man of science, and not merely a petty experimentalist, I should advise you to apply to every branch of natural philosophy, including mathematics.*"

He then took me into his laboratory, and explained to me the uses of his various machines; instructing me as to what I ought to procure, and promising me the use of his own, when I should have advanced far enough in the science not to derange their mechanism.

Thus ended a day memorable to me; it decided my future destiny.

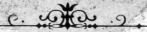

CHAPTER THREE

rom this day natural philosophy became my sole occupation. In M. Waldman I found a true friend. His gentleness was never tinged by dogmatism; and his instructions were given with an air of frankness and good nature, that banished every idea of pedantry. It was, perhaps, the amiable character of this man that inclined me more to that branch of natural philosophy which he professed.

But this state of mind had place only in the first steps towards knowledge: the more fully I entered into the science, the more exclusively I pursued it for its own sake. That application now became so ardent and eager, that the stars often disappeared in the light of morning whilst I was yet engaged in my laboratory.

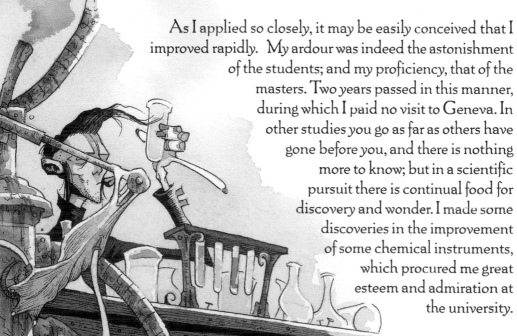

As I applied so closely, it may be easily conceived that I improved rapidly. My ardour was indeed the astonishment of the students; and my proficiency, that of the masters. Two years passed in this manner, during which I paid no visit to Geneva. In other studies you go as far as others have gone before you, and there is nothing more to know; but in a scientific pursuit there is continual food for discovery and wonder. I made some discoveries in the improvement of some chemical instruments, which procured me great esteem and admiration at the university.

One of the phenomena which had peculiarly attracted my attention was the structure of the human frame, and, indeed, any animal endued with life. Whence, I often asked myself, did the principle of life proceed? It was a bold question, and one which has ever been considered as a mystery; yet with how many things are we upon the brink of becoming acquainted, if cowardice or carelessness did not restrain our inquiries. I revolved these circumstances in my mind, and determined thenceforth to apply myself more particularly to those branches of natural philosophy which relate to physiology. To examine the causes of life, we must first have recourse to death. I became acquainted with the science of anatomy: but this was not sufficient; I must also observe the natural decay and corruption of the human body. Darkness had no effect upon my fancy; and a church-yard was to me merely the receptacle of bodies deprived of life, which, from being the seat of beauty and strength, had become food for the worm. Now I was led to examine the cause and progress of this decay, and forced to spend days and nights in vaults and charnel houses. My attention was fixed upon every object the most insupportable to the delicacy of the human feelings. I saw how the fine form of man was degraded and wasted; I beheld the corruption of death succeed to the blooming cheek of life; I saw how the worm inherited the wonders of the eye and brain. I paused, examining and analysing all the minutiae of causation, as exemplified in the change from life to death, and death to life, until from the midst of this darkness a sudden light broke in upon me—a light so brilliant and wondrous, yet so simple, that while I became dizzy with the immensity of the prospect which it illustrated, I was surprised that among so many men of genius, who had directed their inquiries towards the same science, that I alone should be reserved to discover so astonishing a secret.

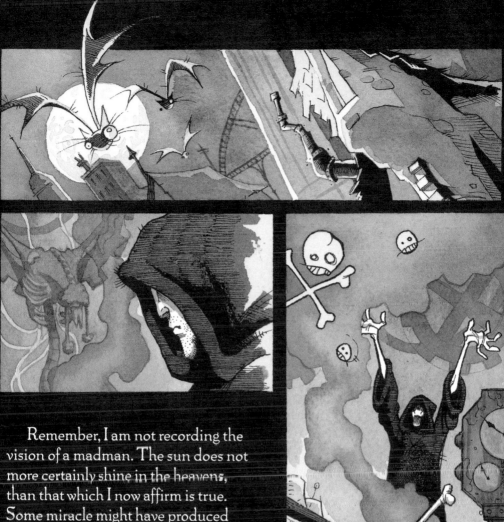

Remember, I am not recording the vision of a madman. The sun does not more certainly shine in the heavens, than that which I now affirm is true. Some miracle might have produced it, yet the stages of the discovery were distinct and probable. After days and nights of incredible labour and fatigue, I succeeded in discovering the cause of generation and life; nay, more, I became myself capable of bestowing animation upon lifeless matter.

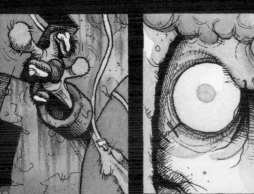

The astonishment which I had at first experienced on this discovery soon gave place to delight and rapture. After so much time spent in painful labour, to arrive at once at the summit of my desires, was the most gratifying consummation of my toils. But this discovery was so great and overwhelming, that all the steps by which I had been progressively led to it were obliterated, and I beheld only the result. What had been the study and desire of the wisest men since the creation of the world, was now within my grasp. I was like the Arabian who had been buried with the dead, and found a passage to life aided only by one glimmering, and seemingly ineffectual, light.

When I found so astonishing a power placed within my hands, I hesitated a long time concerning the manner in which I should employ it. Although I possessed the capacity of bestowing animation, yet to prepare a frame for the reception of it, with all its intricacies of fibres, muscles, and veins, still remained a work of inconceivable difficulty and labour. But my imagination was too much exalted by my first success to permit me to doubt of my ability to give life to an animal as complex and wonderful as man. The materials at present within my command hardly appeared adequate to so arduous an undertaking; but I doubted not that I should ultimately succeed. It was with these feelings that I began the creation of a human being. As the minuteness of the parts formed a great hindrance to my speed, I resolved to make the being of a gigantic stature; about eight feet in height, and proportionably large. After having formed this determination, and having spent some months in successfully collecting and arranging my materials, I began.

No one can conceive the variety of feelings which bore me onwards, like a hurricane, in the first enthusiasm of success. Life and death appeared to me ideal bounds, which I should first break through, and pour a torrent of light into our dark world. I thought that if I could bestow animation upon lifeless matter, I might in process of time renew life where death had apparently devoted the body to corruption.

The moon gazed on my midnight labours, while, with unrelaxed and breathless eagerness, I pursued nature to her hiding places. Who shall conceive the horrors of my secret toil, as I dabbled among the unhallowed damps of the grave?

I seemed to have lost all soul or sensation but for this one pursuit. I collected bones from charnel houses; and disturbed, with profane fingers, the tremendous secrets of the human frame.

In a solitary chamber, or rather cell, at the top of the house, and separated from all the other apartments by a gallery and staircase, I kept my workshop of filthy creation. The dissecting room and the slaughter-house furnished many of my materials; and often did my human nature turn with loathing from my occupation, whilst, still urged on by an eagerness which perpetually increased, I brought my work near to a conclusion.

The summer months passed while I was thus engaged, heart and soul, in one pursuit. It was a most beautiful season; never did the fields bestow a more plentiful harvest, or the vines yield a more luxuriant vintage: but my eyes were insensible to the charms of nature. And the same feelings which made me neglect the scenes around me caused me also to forget those friends who were so many miles absent, and whom I had not seen for so long a time.

I could not tear my thoughts from my employment, loathsome in itself, but which had taken an irresistible hold of my imagination. I wished, as it were, to procrastinate all that related to my feelings of affection until the great object, which swallowed up every habit of my nature, should be completed.

Winter, spring, and summer, passed away during my labours; but I did not watch the blossom or the expanding leaves—sights which before always yielded me supreme delight, so deeply was I engrossed in my occupation. The leaves of that year had withered before my work drew near to a close.

Every night I was oppressed by a slow fever, and I became nervous to a most painful degree; a disease that I regretted the more because I had hitherto enjoyed most excellent health, and had always boasted of the firmness of my nerves. But I believed that exercise and amusement would soon drive away such symptoms; and I promised myself both of these, when my creation should be complete.

It was on a dreary night of November that I beheld the accomplishment of my toils. With an anxiety that almost amounted to agony, I collected the instruments of life around me, that I might infuse a spark of being into the lifeless thing that lay at my feet. The rain pattered dismally against the panes, and my candle was nearly burnt out, when, by the glimmer of the half-extinguished light, I saw the dull yellow eye of the creature open.

How can I describe my emotions at this catastrophe. His limbs were in proportion, and I had selected his features as beautiful. Beautiful!— Great God! His yellow skin scarcely covered the work of muscles and arteries beneath; his hair was of a lustrous black, and flowing; his teeth of a pearly whiteness; but these luxuriances only formed a more horrid contrast with his watery eyes, that seemed almost of the same colour as the dun white sockets in which they were set, his shrivelled complexion, and straight black lips.

The different accidents of life are not so changeable as the feelings of human nature. I had worked hard for nearly two years, for the sole purpose of infusing life into an inanimate body. For this I had deprived myself of rest and health. I had desired it with an ardour that far exceeded moderation; but now that I had finished, the beauty of the dream vanished, and breathless horror and disgust filled my heart.

Unable to endure the aspect of the being I had created, I rushed out of the room, and threw myself on the bed in my clothes, endeavouring to seek a few moments of forgetfulness.

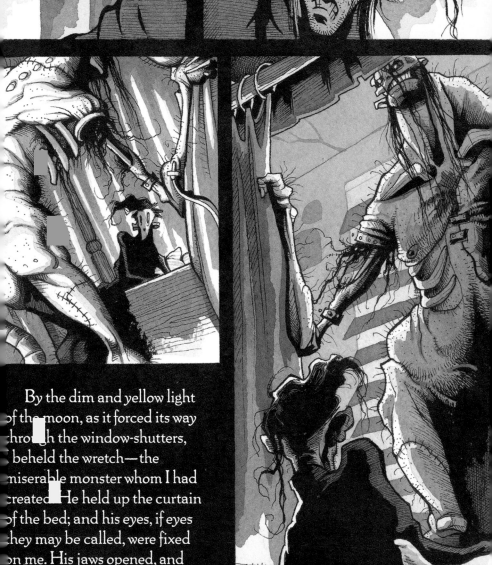

By the dim and yellow light of the moon, as it forced its way through the window-shutters, I beheld the wretch—the miserable monster whom I had created. He held up the curtain of the bed; and his eyes, if eyes they may be called, were fixed on me. His jaws opened, and he muttered some inarticulate sounds.

I took refuge in the court-yard belonging to the house which I inhabited; where I remained during the rest of the night, walking up and down in the greatest agitation, listening attentively, catching and fearing each sound as if it were to announce the approach of the demoniacal corpse to which I had so miserably given life.

I passed the night wretchedly. I felt the bitterness of disappointment: dreams that had been my food and pleasant rest for so long a space, were now become a hell to me.

Morning, dismal and wet, at length dawned, and discovered to my sleepless and aching eyes the church of Ingolstadt, its white steeple and clock, which indicated the sixth hour.

I issued into the streets, pacing them with quick steps, as if I sought to avoid the wretch whom I feared every turning of the street would present to my view. I did not dare return to the apartment which I inhabited.

Like one who, on a lonely road,
Doth walk in fear and dread,
And, having once turn'd round, walks on,
And turns no more his head;
Because he knows a frightful fiend
Doth close behind him tread.

"My dear Frankenstein, how glad I am to see you!

"How fortunate that you should be here at the very moment of my alighting!"

I grasped Henry Clerval's hand, and in a moment forgot my horror and misfortune; I felt suddenly, and for the first time during many months, calm and serene joy. I welcomed my friend, therefore, in the most cordial manner, and we walked towards my college.

"It gives me the greatest delight to see you; but tell me how you left my father, brothers, and Elizabeth."

"Very well, and very happy, only a little uneasy that they hear from you so seldom. But, my dear Frankenstein, I did not before remark how very ill you appear; so thin and pale."

"I have lately been so deeply engaged in one occupation, that I have not allowed myself sufficient rest, as you see: but I hope, I sincerely hope, that all these employments are now at an end, and that I am at length free."

I trembled excessively; I could not endure to think of, and far less to allude to the occurrences of the preceding night. The thought made me shiver, that the creature whom I had left in my apartment might still be there, alive, and walking about. I dreaded to behold this monster; but I feared still more that Henry should see him. I darted up towards my own room.

My hand was already on the lock of the door before I recollected myself. I then paused; and a cold shivering came over me. I threw the door forcibly open, but nothing appeared. The apartment was empty. I could hardly believe that so great a good-fortune could have befallen me.

We ascended into my room; I was unable to contain myself. Clerval saw a wildness in my eyes for which he could not account; and my loud, unrestrained, heartless laughter, frightened and astonished him.

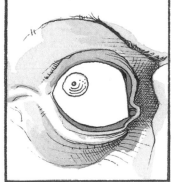

"My dear Victor, what, for God's sake, is the matter? Do not laugh in that manner. How ill you are!"

"Oh, save me! save me!"

This was the commencement of a nervous fever, which confined me for several months. During all that time Henry was my only nurse.

The form of the monster on whom I had bestowed existence was for ever before my eyes, and I raved incessantly.

CHAPTER FIVE

My Dear Cousin,

I cannot describe to you the uneasiness we have all felt concerning your health. We cannot help imagining that your friend Clerval conceals the extent of your disorder. He always writes that you are getting better; I eagerly hope that you will confirm this intelligence soon in your own hand-writing; for indeed, indeed, Victor, we are all very miserable on this account. Relieve us from this fear, and we shall be the happiest creatures in the world. Your father's health is now so vigorous, that he appears ten years younger since last winter. Ernest also is so much improved, that you would hardly know him: he is now nearly sixteen, and has lost that sickly appearance which he had some years ago; he is grown quite robust and active.

My uncle and I conversed a long time last night about what profession Ernest should follow. Now that he enjoys good health, he is continually in the open air, climbing the hills, or rowing on the lake. I therefore proposed that he should be a farmer; which you know, Cousin, is a favourite scheme of mine. My uncle had an idea of his being educated as an advocate, that through his interest he might become a judge. I said, that the employments of a prosperous farmer, if they were not a more honourable, they were at least a happier species of occupation than that of a judge, whose misfortune it was always to meddle with the dark side of human nature.

And now I must tell you a little story that will please, and perhaps amuse you. Do you not remember Justine Moritz? Madame Moritz, her mother, was a widow with four children, of whom Justine was the third. Her mother could not endure her, and, after the death of M. Moritz, treated her very ill. My aunt observed this; and, when Justine was twelve years of age, prevailed on her mother to allow her to live at her house. Justine, thus received in our family, learned the duties of a servant; a condition which, in our fortunate country, does not include the idea of ignorance, and a sacrifice of the dignity of a human being.

After what I have said, I dare say you well remember the heroine of my little tale: for Justine was a great favourite of yours. One by one, her brothers and sister died; and her mother, with the exception of her neglected daughter, was left childless. The conscience of the woman was troubled; she began to think that the deaths of her favourites was a judgment from heaven to chastise her partiality. She was a Roman Catholic; and I believe her confessor confirmed the idea which she had conceived. She sometimes begged Justine to forgive her unkindness, but much oftener accused her of having caused the deaths of her brothers and sister. Perpetual fretting at length threw Madame Moritz into a decline. She died on the first approach of cold weather, at the beginning of this last winter. Justine has returned to us; and I assure you I love her tenderly. She is very clever and gentle, and extremely pretty; as I mentioned before, her mien and her expressions continually remind me of my dear aunt.

I must say also a few words to you, my dear cousin, of little darling William. I wish you could see him; he is very tall of his age, with sweet laughing blue eyes, dark eye-lashes, and curling hair. When he smiles, two little dimples appear on each cheek, which are rosy with health.

I have written myself into good spirits, dear cousin; yet I cannot conclude without again anxiously inquiring concerning your health. Dear Victor, if you are not very ill, write yourself, and make your father and all of us happy; or — I cannot bear to think of the other side of the question; my tears already flow. Adieu, my dearest cousin.

Elizabeth Lavenza

Geneva, March 18th

CHAPTER SIX

My Dear Victor,

You have probably waited impatiently for a letter to fix the date of your return to us; and I was at first tempted to write only a few lines, merely mentioning the day on which I should expect you. What would be your surprise, my son, when you expected a happy and gay welcome, to behold, on the contrary, tears and wretchedness?

William is dead!—that sweet child, whose smiles delighted and warmed my heart, who was so gentle, yet so gay! Victor, he is murdered!

I will not attempt to console you; but will simply relate the circumstances of the transaction.

Last Thursday (May 7th) I, my niece, and your two brothers, went to walk in Plainpalais. The evening was warm and serene, and we prolonged our walk farther than usual. It was already dusk before we discovered that William and Ernest, who had gone on before, were not to be found. Ernest came, and said that they had been playing together, that William had run away to hide himself, and did not return.

This account rather alarmed us, and we continued to search for him with torches; for I could not rest, when I thought that my sweet boy had lost himself, and was exposed to all the damps and dews of night. About five in the morning I discovered my lovely boy, whom the night before I had seen blooming and active in health, stretched on the grass livid and motionless: the print of the murderer's finger was on his neck.

He was conveyed home, and the anguish that was visible in my countenance betrayed the secret to Elizabeth. She was very earnest to see the corpse. Entering the room where it lay, she hastily examined the neck of the victim, and clasping her hands exclaimed, 'O God! I have murdered my darling infant!'

She told me, that that same evening William had teazed her to let him wear a very valuable miniature that she possessed of your mother. This picture is gone, and was doubtless the temptation which urged the murderer to the deed.

Come, dearest Victor; you alone can console Elizabeth. She weeps continually, and accuses herself unjustly as the cause of his death; her words pierce my heart.

Your affectionate and afflicted father,

Alphonse Frankenstein
Geneva, May 12th

"*My dear Frankenstein, are you always to be unhappy? My dear friend, what has happened?*"

"*I can offer you no consolation, my friend, your disaster is irreparable. What do you intend to do?*"

"*To go instantly to Geneva.*"

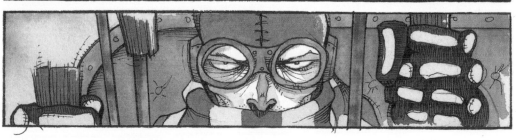

It was completely dark when I arrived in the environs of Geneva. The sky was serene; and, as I was unable to rest, I resolved to visit the spot where my poor William had been murdered.

During this short voyage I saw the lightnings playing on the summit of Mont Blanc in the most beautiful figures.

The storm appeared to approach rapidly; I ascended a low hill, that I might observe its progress. It advanced; the heavens were clouded, and I soon felt the rain coming slowly in large drops, but its violence quickly increased.

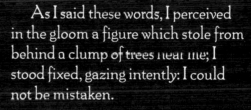

"William, dear angel! this is thy funeral, this thy dirge!"

As I said these words, I perceived in the gloom a figure which stole from behind a clump of trees near me; I stood fixed, gazing intently: I could not be mistaken.

A flash of lightning illuminated the object, and discovered its shape plainly to me; its gigantic stature, and the deformity of its aspect, more hideous than belongs to humanity, instantly informed me that it was the wretch, the filthy demon to whom I had given life. Could he be the murderer of my brother? He was the murderer!

I thought of pursuing the devil; but it would have been in vain, for another flash discovered him to me hanging among the rocks of the nearly perpendicular ascent of Mont Salêve. He soon reached the summit, and disappeared.

Two years had now nearly elapsed since the night on which he first received life; and was this his first crime? Alas! I had turned loose into the world a depraved wretch, whose delight was in carnage and misery.

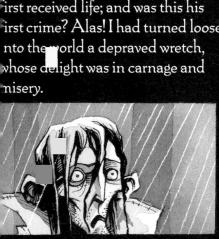

The remainder of the night I spent, cold and wet, in the open air. My imagination was busy in scenes of evil and despair. I considered the being whom I had cast among mankind, and endowed with the will and power to effect purposes of horror, and forced to destroy all that was dear to me.

Day dawned; and I hastened to my father's house. My first thought was to discover what I knew of the murderer, and cause instant pursuit to be made. But I paused when I reflected on the story that I had to tell. I remembered also the nervous fever with which I had been seized just at the time that I dated my creation, and which would give an air of delirium to a tale otherwise so utterly improbable.

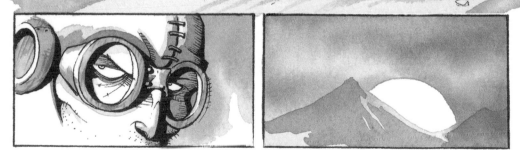

Besides, of what use would be pursuit? Who could arrest a creature capable of scaling the overhanging sides of Mont Salêve? These reflections determined me, and I resolved to remain silent.

"Welcome, my dearest Victor. I wish you had come three months ago, and then you would have found us all joyous and delighted. But we are now unhappy; and, I am afraid, tears instead of smiles will be your welcome."

"Do not welcome me thus; try to be more calm, that I may not be absolutely miserable the moment I enter my father's house after so long an absence. How is my poor Elizabeth?"

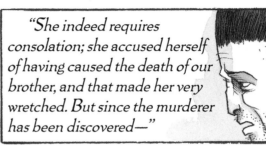

"She indeed requires consolation; she accused herself of having caused the death of our brother, and that made her very wretched. But since the murderer has been discovered—"

"The murderer discovered! Good God! how can that be?"

"Indeed, who would credit that Justine Moritz, who was so amiable, and fond of all the family, could all at once become so extremely wicked?"

"Justine Moritz!"

He related that, the morning on which the murder of poor William had been discovered, Justine had been taken ill, and confined to her bed; and, after several days, one of the servants had discovered in her pocket the picture of my mother, which had been judged to be the temptation of the murderer.

I was firmly convinced in my own mind that Justine, and indeed every human being, was guiltless of this murder. I had no fear, therefore, that any circumstantial evidence could be brought forward strong enough to convict her.

e passed a few sad hours, until eleven o'clock, when the trial was to commence. My father and the rest of the family being obliged to attend as witnesses, I accompanied them to the court. During the whole of this wretched mockery of justice, I suffered living torture. It was to be decided whether the result of my curiosity and lawless devices would cause the death of two of my fellow-beings: one a smiling babe, full of innocence and joy; the other far more dreadfully murdered, with every aggravation of infamy that could make the murder memorable in horror.

The appearance of Justine was calm. She appeared confident in innocence, and did not tremble, for all the kindness which her beauty might otherwise have excited was obliterated in the minds of the spectators by the imagination of the enormity she was supposed to have committed. A tear seemed to dim her eye when she saw us; but she quickly recovered herself, and a look of sorrowful affection seemed to attest her utter guiltlessness.

The trial began; and after the advocate against her had stated the charge, several witnesses were called. Several strange facts combined against her, which might have staggered any one who had not such proof of her innocence as I had.

She had been out the whole of the night on which the murder had been committed, and towards morning had been perceived by a market-woman not far from the spot where the body of the murdered child had been afterwards found. She returned to the house about eight o'clock; and when one inquired where she had passed the night, she replied that she had been looking for the child. When shewn the body, she fell into violent hysterics, and kept her bed for several days. The picture was then produced, which the servant had found in her pocket; and when Elizabeth, in a faltering voice, proved that it was the same which, an hour before the child had been missed, she had placed round his neck, a murmur of horror and indignation filled the court.

"God knows how entirely I am innocent. But I do not pretend that my protestations should acquit me: I rest my innocence on a plain and simple explanation of the facts which have been adduced against me; and I hope the character I have always borne will incline my judges to a favourable interpretation, where any circumstance appears doubtful or suspicious."

She then related that she had passed the evening at the house of an aunt. On her return, she met a man, who asked her if she had seen any thing of the child who was lost. She was alarmed, and passed several hours in looking for him. That she had been bewildered when questioned by the market-woman was not surprising, since she had passed a sleepless night. Concerning the picture she could give no account.

"I know how heavily and fatally this one circumstance weighs against me, but I have no power of explaining it. I believe that I have no enemy on earth, and none surely would have been so wicked as to destroy me wantonly. I commit my cause to the justice of my judges, yet I see no room for hope. I beg permission to have a few witnesses examined concerning my character; and if their testimony shall not overweigh my supposed guilt, I must be condemned, although I would pledge my salvation on my innocence."

Several witnesses were called, but fear, and hatred of the crime of which they supposed her guilty, rendered them unwilling to come forward. Elizabeth saw even this last resource about to fail the accused when she desired permission to address the court.

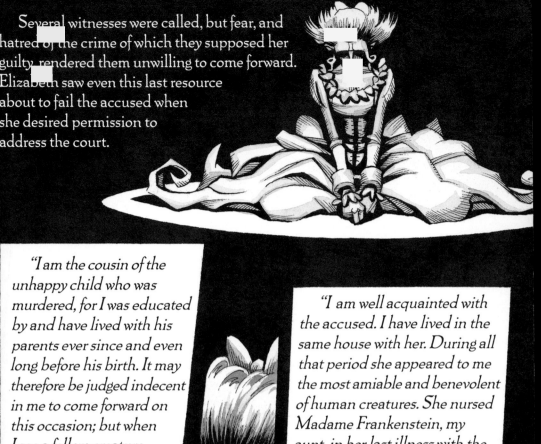

"I am the cousin of the unhappy child who was murdered, for I was educated by and have lived with his parents ever since and even long before his birth. It may therefore be judged indecent in me to come forward on this occasion; but when I see a fellow-creature about to perish through the cowardice of her pretended friends, I wish to be allowed to speak, that I may say what I know of her character.

"I am well acquainted with the accused. I have lived in the same house with her. During all that period she appeared to me the most amiable and benevolent of human creatures. She nursed Madame Frankenstein, my aunt, in her last illness with the greatest affection and care; and afterwards attended her own mother during a tedious illness. She was warmly attached to the child who is now dead, and acted towards him like a most affectionate mother. For my own part, I do not hesitate to say, that, notwithstanding all the evidence produced against her, I believe and rely on her perfect innocence."

Could the demon who had murdered my brother also in his hellish sport have betrayed the innocent to death and ignominy? When I perceived that the popular voice had already condemned my unhappy victim, I rushed out of the court in agony. The tortures of the accused did not equal mine; she was sustained by innocence, but the fangs of remorse tore my bosom, and would not forego their hold.

The ballots had been thrown; they were all black, and Justine was condemned.

Words cannot convey an idea of the heart-sickening despair that I then endured.

Soon after we heard that the poor victim had expressed a wish to see my cousin.

We entered the gloomy prison-chamber, and beheld Justine. She threw herself at the feet of Elizabeth, weeping bitterly. My cousin wept also.

"Do you also believe that I am so very, very wicked? Do you also join with my enemies to crush me?"

Her voice was suffocated with sobs.

"Rise, my poor girl, why do you kneel, if you are innocent? I believe you guiltless."

"I confessed! The God of heaven forgive me!

"Ever since I was condemned, my confessor has besieged me.

"He threatened and menaced, until I almost began to think that I was the monster that he said I was. He threatened excommunication and hell fire in my last moments. What could I do? In an evil hour I subscribed to a lie.

"Dear William! dearest blessed child! I soon shall see you again in heaven, where we shall all be happy."

"Heaven bless thee, my dearest Justine, with resignation, and a confidence elevated beyond this world. Oh! how I hate its shews and mockeries! when one creature is murdered, another is immediately deprived of life in a slow torturing manner; then the executioners, their hands yet reeking with the blood of innocence, believe that they have done a great deed. They call this retribution. Hateful name! I would I were in peace with my aunt and my lovely William, escaped from a world which is hateful to me, and the visages of men which I abhor."

I had retired to a corner of the prison-room, where I could conceal the horrid anguish that possessed me. The poor victim, who on the morrow was to pass the dreary boundary between life and death, felt not as I did, such deep and bitter agony. I gnashed my teeth, and ground them together, uttering a groan that came from my inmost soul. The poor sufferer gained the resignation she desired. But I, the true murderer, felt the never-dying worm alive in my bosom,

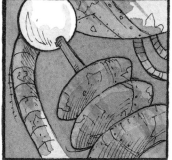
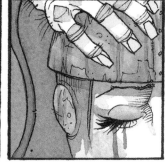

which allowed of no hope or consolation. Elizabeth also wept, and was unhappy; but hers also was the misery of innocence, which, like a cloud that passes over the fair moon, for a while hides, but cannot tarnish its brightness. Anguish and despair had penetrated into the core of my heart; I bore a hell within me, which nothing could extinguish.

I was a wretch, and none ever conceived of the misery that I then endured.

VOLUME
II

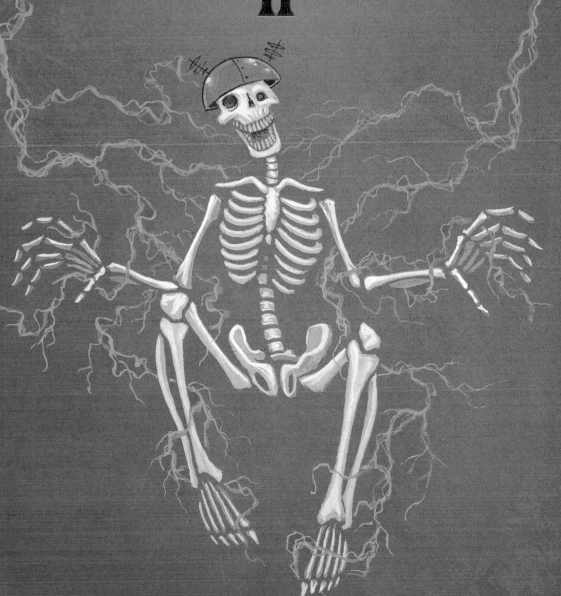

CHAPTER ONE

Nothing is more painful to the human mind than, after the feelings have been worked up by a quick succession of events, the dead calmness of inaction and certainty which follows, and deprives the soul both of hope and fear.

Justine died; and I was alive. The blood flowed freely in my veins, but a weight of despair and remorse pressed on my heart, which nothing could remove. Sleep fled from my eyes; I wandered like an evil spirit, for I had committed deeds of mischief beyond description horrible.

I was seized by remorse and the sense of guilt, which hurried me away to a hell of intense tortures such as no language can describe.

This state of mind preyed upon my health, which had entirely recovered from the first shock it had sustained. I shunned the face of man; all sound of joy or complacency was torture to me; solitude was my only consolation—deep, dark, death-like solitude.

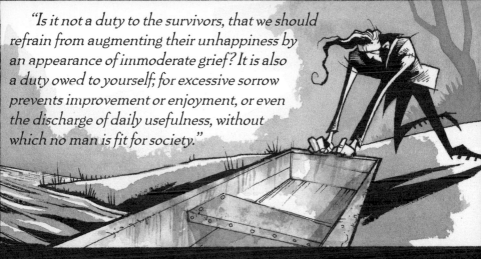

"Is it not a duty to the survivors, that we should refrain from augmenting their unhappiness by an appearance of immoderate grief? It is also a duty owed to yourself; for excessive sorrow prevents improvement or enjoyment, or even the discharge of daily usefulness, without which no man is fit for society."

I could only answer my father with a look of despair, and endeavour to hide myself from his view.

Often, after the rest of the family had retired for the night, I took the boat and passed many hours upon the water. I was often tempted, when all was at peace around me, and I the only unquiet thing that wandered restless in a scene so beautiful and heavenly, to plunge into the silent lake, that the waters might close over me and my calamities for ever. But I was restrained when I thought of the heroic and suffering Elizabeth, whom I tenderly loved, and whose existence was bound up in mine.

At these moments I wept bitterly, and wished that peace would revisit my mind only that I might afford them consolation and happiness. But that could not be. Remorse extinguished every hope. I had been the author of unalterable evils; and I lived in daily fear, lest the monster whom I had created should perpetrate some new wickedness. I had an obscure feeling that all was not over. When I thought of him, I gnashed my teeth, my eyes became inflamed, and I ardently wished to extinguish that life which I had so thoughtlessly bestowed.

I wished to see him again, that I might wreak the utmost extent of anger on his head, and avenge the deaths of William and Justine.

Our house was the house of mourning. My father's health was deeply shaken by the horror of the recent events. Elizabeth was sad and desponding.

"When I reflect, my dear cousin, on the miserable death of Justine Moritz, I no longer see the world and its works as they before appeared to me. Misery has come home, and men appear to me as monsters thirsting for each other's blood. Alas! Victor, when falsehood can look so like the truth, who can assure themselves of certain happiness? William and Justine were assassinated, and the murderer escapes. But even if I were condemned to suffer on the scaffold for the same crimes, I would not change places with such a wretch."

I listened to this discourse with the extremest agony. I, not in deed, but in effect, was the true murderer.

My father, who saw in the unhappiness that was painted in my face only an exaggeration of that sorrow which I might naturally feel, proposed that we should all make an excursion to the valley of Chamounix. Accordingly we departed from Geneva on this tour about the middle of the month of August, nearly two months after the death of Justine.

The weather was uncommonly fine; and if mine had been a sorrow to be chased away by any fleeting circumstance, this excursion would certainly have had the effect intended by my father.

We perceived that the valley through which we wound, and which was formed by the river Arve, whose course we followed, closed in upon us by degrees; and when the sun had set, we beheld immense mountains and precipices overhanging us on every side, and heard the sound of the river raging among rocks, and the dashing of waterfalls around.

Mont Blanc, the supreme and magnificent Mont Blanc, raised itself from the surrounding aiguilles, and its tremendous dome overlooked the valley.

We retired early to our apartments, but not to sleep; at least I did not.

CHAPTER TWO

These sublime and magnificent scenes afforded me the greatest consolation that I was capable of receiving. Although they did not remove my grief, they subdued and tranquillized it. In some degree, also, they diverted my mind from the thoughts over which it had brooded for the last month. My father was pleased, and Elizabeth overjoyed.

"My dear cousin, you see what happiness you diffuse when you are happy; do not relapse again!"

The following morning the rain poured down in torrents, and thick mists hid the summits of the mountains. I rose early, but felt unusually melancholy. The rain depressed me; my old feelings recurred, and I was miserable. I knew how disappointed my father would be at this sudden change, and resolved to go alone to the summit of Montanvert. I remembered the effect that the view of the tremendous and ever-moving glacier had produced upon my mind when I first saw it. It had then filled me with a sublime ecstacy that gave wings to the soul.

Alas! why does man boast of sensibilities superior to those apparent in the brute; it only renders them more necessary beings. If our impulses were confined to hunger, thirst, and desire, we might be nearly free; but now we are moved by every wind that blows, and a chance word or scene that that word may convey to us.

"Wandering spirits, if indeed ye wander and do not rest in your narrow beds, allow me this faint happiness, or take me, as your companion, away from the joys of life."

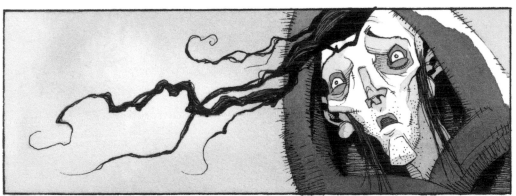

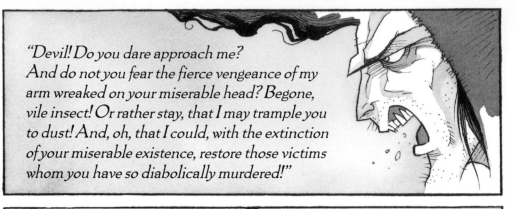

"Devil! Do you dare approach me? And do not you fear the fierce vengeance of my arm wreaked on your miserable head? Begone, vile insect! Or rather stay, that I may trample you to dust! And, oh, that I could, with the extinction of your miserable existence, restore those victims whom you have so diabolically murdered!"

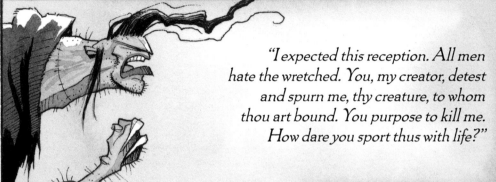

"I expected this reception. All men hate the wretched. You, my creator, detest and spurn me, thy creature, to whom thou art bound. You purpose to kill me. How dare you sport thus with life?"

"Abhorred monster! Fiend that thou art! The tortures of hell are too mild a vengeance for thy crimes. Wretched devil! Come on then, that I may extinguish the spark which I so negligently bestowed."

"Have I not suffered enough, that you seek to increase my misery? Life, although it may only be an accumulation of anguish, is dear to me, and I will defend it.

"Remember, thou hast made me more powerful than thyself. But I will not be tempted to set myself in opposition to thee. I am thy creature: I ought to be thy Adam; but I am rather the fallen angel whom thou drivest from joy for no misdeed."

"Begone! I will not hear you. There can be no community between you and me; we are enemies. Begone, or let us try our strength in a fight, in which one must fall."

"How can I move thee? Believe me, Frankenstein: I was benevolent; my soul glowed with love and humanity: but am I not alone, miserably alone?"

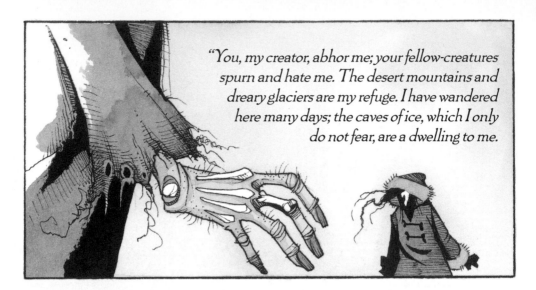

"You, my creator, abhor me; your fellow-creatures spurn and hate me. The desert mountains and dreary glaciers are my refuge. I have wandered here many days; the caves of ice, which I only do not fear, are a dwelling to me.

"If the multitude of mankind knew of my existence, they would do as you do, and arm themselves for my destruction. Shall I not then hate them who abhor me? Listen to my tale. The guilty are allowed, by human laws, bloody as they may be, to speak in their own defence before they are condemned. Listen to me, Frankenstein. You accuse me of murder; and yet you would, with a satisfied conscience, destroy your own creature. I ask you not to spare me: listen to me; and then, if you can, and if you will, destroy the work of your hands."

"Cursed be the day, abhorred devil, in which you first saw light! Cursed be the hands that formed you! You have made me wretched beyond expression. Begone! relieve me from the sight of your detested form."

"Hear my tale; On you it rests, whether I quit forever the neighbourhood of man and lead a harmless life, or become the scourge of your fellow-creatures and the author of your own speedy ruin."

For the first time I felt what the duties of a creator towards his creature were.

CHAPTER THREE

"It is with considerable difficulty that I remember the original aera of my being. I saw, felt, heard, and smelt, at the same time; and it was, indeed, a long time before I learned to distinguish between the operations of my various senses.

"It was dark when I awoke...."

CHAPTER FOUR

"I lay on my straw, but I could not sleep. What chiefly struck me was the gentle manners of these people; and I longed to join them, but dared not. I remembered too well the treatment I had suffered from the barbarous villagers, and resolved that for the present I would remain quietly in my hovel, watching, and endeavouring to discover the motives which influenced their actions."

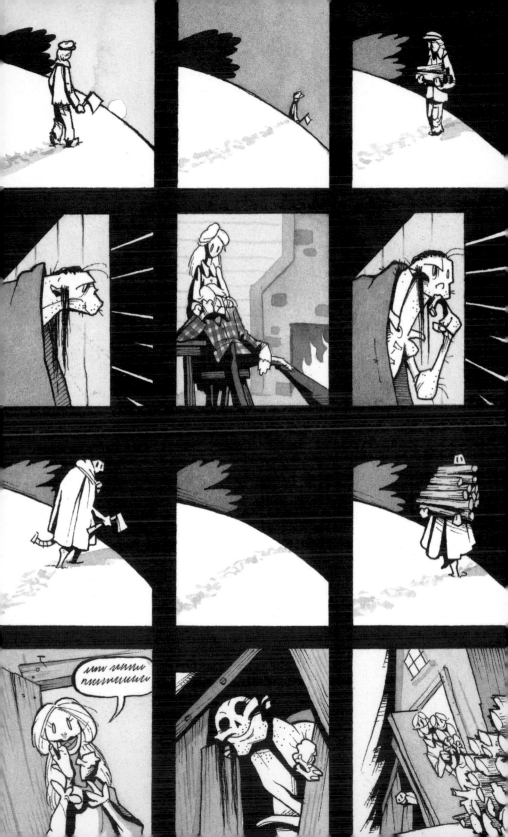

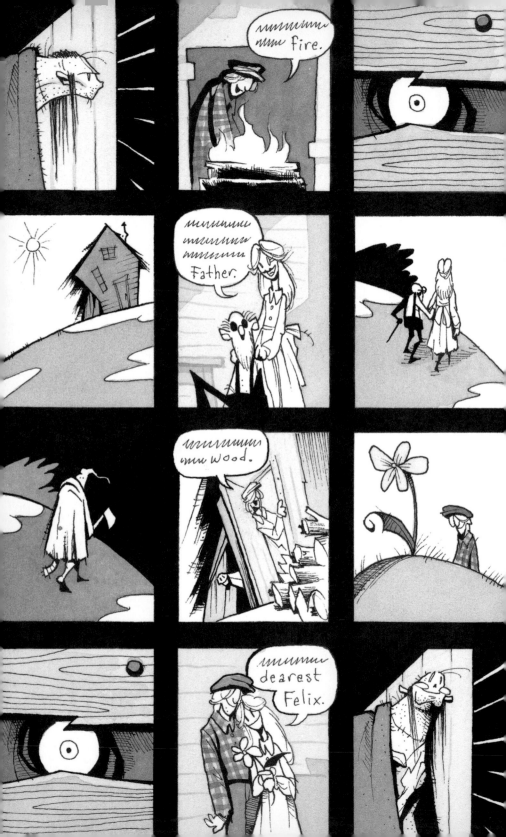

"My spirits were elevated by the enchanting appearance of nature; the past was blotted from my memory, the present was tranquil, and the future gilded by bright rays of hope, and anticipations of joy.

"Of what a strange nature is knowledge! It clings to the mind, when it has once seized on it, like a lichen on the rock. I wished sometimes to shake off all thought and feeling; but I learned that there was but one means to overcome the sensation of pain, and that was death."

CHAPTER FIVE

"**I** learned, from the views of social life, to admire their virtues, and to deprecate the vices of mankind. As yet I looked upon crime as a distant evil; benevolence and generosity were ever present before me."

As I read, I applied much personally to my own feelings and condition. I found myself similar, yet at the same time strangely unlike the beings concerning whom I read, and to whose conversation I was a listener. I sympathized with, and partly understood them, but I was unformed in mind; I was dependent on none, and related to none. My person was hideous, and my stature gigantic: what did this mean?

JOURNAL

hatefull day
hen I received
Life !!!

"Cursed Creator!

"Why did you form a monster so hideous that even you turned from me in disgust?"

"Increase of knowledge only discovered to me more clearly what a wretched outcast I was. I cherished hope, it is true; but it vanished, when I beheld my person reflected in water, or my shadow in the moon-shine. I endeavored to crush these fears."

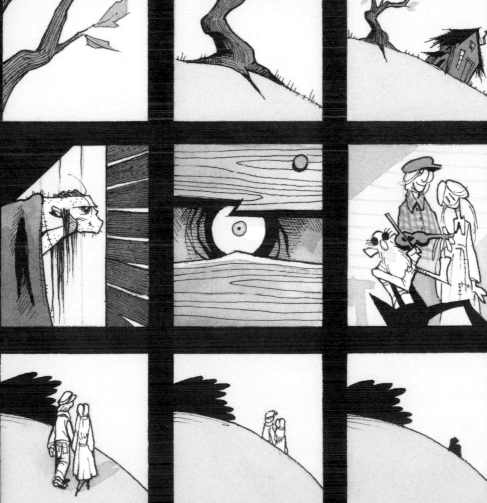

*"Who is there?
Come in."*

*"Pardon this intrusion, I
am a traveller in want of
a little rest."*

*"Enter, and I will try
in what manner I can
relieve your wants; but,
unfortunately, my children
are from home, and, as I am
blind, I am afraid I shall
find it difficult to procure
food for you."*

*"Do not trouble yourself, my kind host, I have food; it
is warmth and rest only that I need. I am now going to
claim the protection of some friends, whom I sincerely
love, and of whose favour I have some hopes. I am an
unfortunate and deserted creature; I look around, and
I have no relation or friend upon earth. These amiable
people to whom I go have never seen me, and know
little of me. I am full of fears; for if I fail there, I am an
outcast in the world for ever."*

*"Do not despair. To be friendless is indeed to
be unfortunate; but the hearts of men are full of
brotherly love and charity. Rely, therefore, on your
hopes; and if these friends are good and amiable,
do not despair."*

"They are kind—they are the most excellent creatures in the world; but a fatal prejudice clouds their eyes, and where they ought to see a feeling and kind friend, they behold only a detestable monster."

"That is indeed unfortunate; but if you are really blameless, cannot you undeceive them?"

"I am about to undertake that task; and it is on that account that I feel so many overwhelming terrors. I tenderly love these friends; I have, unknown to them, been for many months in the habits of daily kindness towards them; but they believe that I wish to injure them, and it is that prejudice which I wish to overcome."

"Where do these friends reside?"

"Near this spot."

"If you will unreservedly confide to me the particulars of your tale, I perhaps may be of use in undeceiving them. I am blind and cannot judge of your countenance, but there is something in your words which persuades me that you are sincere."

"I thank you, and accept your generous offer. You raise me from the dust by this kindness; and I trust that, by your aid, I shall not be driven from the society and sympathy of your fellow-creatures."

"May I know the names and residence of those friends?"

"You and your family are the friends whom I seek."

"Overcome by pain and anguish, I quitted the cottage."

CHAPTER SIX

"Cursed, cursed creator! Why, in that instant, did I not extinguish the spark of existence which you had so wantonly bestowed?"

"Ugly wretch! You wish to eat me."

"Child, I do not intend to hurt you."

"Hideous monster! let me go; My papa is M. Frankenstein—he would punish you."

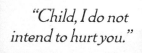

"My enemy is not impregnable; this death will carry despair to him, and a thousand other miseries shall destroy him."

"At length I wandered towards these mountains, and have ranged through their immense recesses, consumed by a burning passion which you alone can gratify. We may not part until you have promised to comply with my requisition. I am alone, and miserable; man will not associate with me; but one as deformed and horrible as myself would not deny herself to me. My companion must be of the same species, and have the same defects. This being you must create."

CHAPTER SEVEN

The being finished speaking, and fixed his looks upon me in expectation of a reply. But I was bewildered, perplexed, and unable to arrange my ideas sufficiently to understand the full extent of his proposition.

"You must create a female for me, with whom I can live in the interchange of those sympathies necessary for my being. I demand it of you as a right which you must not refuse."

The latter part of his tale had kindled anew in me the anger that had died away while he narrated his peaceful life among the cottagers. I could no longer suppress the rage that burned within me.

"I do refuse it. Shall I create another like yourself, whose joint wickedness might desolate the world? Begone! I have answered you; you may torture me, but I will never consent."

"You are in the wrong. I am malicious because I am miserable. You, my creator, would tear me to pieces, and destroy my frame, the work of your own hands. Shall I respect man, when he contemns me? If I cannot inspire love, I will cause fear; and work at your destruction, nor finish until I desolate your heart, so that you curse the hour of your birth."

"What I ask of you is reasonable and moderate; I demand a creature of another sex, but as hideous as myself: we shall be monsters, cut off from all the world; but on that account we shall be more attached to one another. Our lives will be harmless, and free from the misery I now feel. Oh! my creator, make me happy; do not deny me my request!"

I was moved. I shuddered when I thought of the possible consequences of my consent; but I felt that there was some justice in his argument. His tale, and the feelings he now expressed, proved him to be a creature of fine sensations; and did I not, as his maker, owe him all the portion of happiness that it was in my power to bestow?

"If you consent, neither you nor any other human being shall ever see us again: I will go to the vast wilds of South America. We shall make our bed of dried leaves; the sun will shine on us as on man, and will ripen our food. The picture I present to you is peaceful and human, and you must feel that you could deny it only in the wantonness of power and cruelty. Pitiless as you have been towards me, I now see compassion in your eyes."

"I swear to you that, with the companion you bestow, I will quit the neighbourhood of man. My evil passions will have fled, for I shall meet with sympathy; my life will flow quietly away, and, in my dying moments, I shall not curse my maker."

When I looked upon him, when I saw the filthy mass that moved and talked, my heart sickened. I tried to stifle these sensations; as I could not sympathize with him, I had no right to withhold from him the small portion of happiness which was yet in my power to bestow.

"The love of another will destroy the cause of my crimes. My vices are the children of a forced solitude that I abhor; and my virtues will necessarily arise when I live in communion with an equal. I shall feel the affections of a sensitive being, and become linked to the chain of existence and events, from which I am now excluded."

After a long pause of reflection, I concluded, that the justice due both to him and my fellow-creatures demanded of me that I should comply with his request.

"I consent to your demand, on your solemn oath to quit Europe for ever, and every other place in the neighbourhood of man, as soon as I shall deliver into your hands a female who will accompany you in your exile."

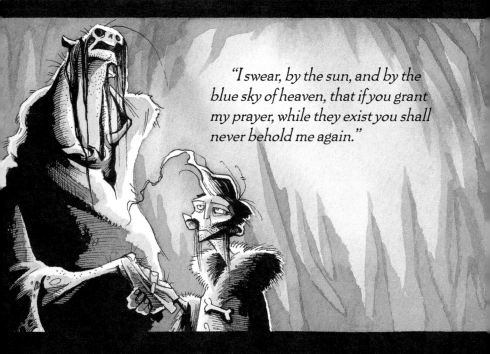

"I swear, by the sun, and by the blue sky of heaven, that if you grant my prayer, while they exist you shall never behold me again."

He suddenly quitted me, fearful, perhaps, of any change in my sentiments. I saw him descend the mountain with greater speed than the flight of an eagle, and quickly lost him among the undulations of the sea of ice.

His tale had occupied the whole day; and the sun was upon the verge of the horizon when he departed. I knew that I ought to hasten my descent towards the valley, as I should soon be encompassed in darkness; but my heart was heavy, and my steps slow. The labour of winding among the little paths of the mountains, and fixing my feet firmly as I advanced, perplexed me, occupied as I was by the emotions which the occurrences of the day had produced.

"Oh! stars, and clouds, and winds, ye are all about to mock me: if ye really pity me, crush sensation and memory; let me become as nought; but if not, depart, depart and leave me in darkness."

The eternal twinkling of the stars weighed upon me. I listened to every blast of wind, as if it were a dull ugly siroc on its way to consume me.

VOLUME
III

CHAPTER ONE

Day after day, week after week, passed away on my return to Geneva; and I could not collect the courage to recommence my work. I feared the vengeance of the disappointed fiend, yet I was unable to overcome my repugnance to the task which was enjoined me. I found that I could not compose a female without again devoting several months to profound study and laborious disquisition.

I had heard of some discoveries having been made by an English philosopher, the knowledge of which was material to my success, and I sometimes thought of obtaining my father's consent to visit England for this purpose; but I clung to every pretence of delay, and could not resolve to interrupt my returning tranquillity.

My health, which had hitherto declined, was now much restored; and my spirits, when unchecked by the memory of my unhappy promise, rose proportionably. My father saw this change with pleasure, and he turned his thoughts towards the best method of eradicating the remains of my melancholy, which every now and then would return by fits, and with a devouring blackness overcast the approaching sunshine.

At these moments I took refuge in the most perfect solitude. I passed whole days on the lake alone in a little boat, watching the clouds, and listening to the rippling of the waves, silent and listless.

It was after my return from one of these rambles that my father, calling me aside, thus addressed me—

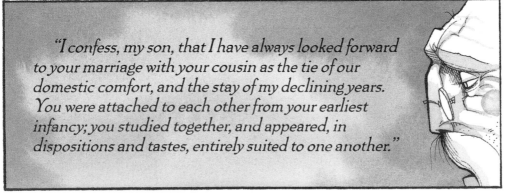

"I confess, my son, that I have always looked forward to your marriage with your cousin as the tie of our domestic comfort, and the stay of my declining years. You were attached to each other from your earliest infancy; you studied together, and appeared, in dispositions and tastes, entirely suited to one another."

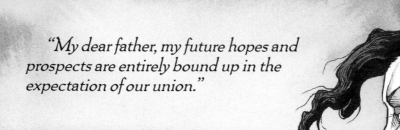

"My dear father, my future hopes and prospects are entirely bound up in the expectation of our union."

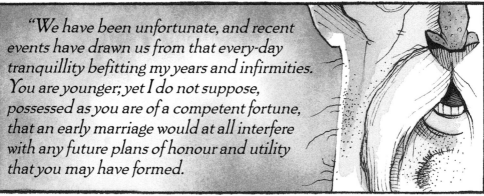

"The expression of your sentiments on this subject, my dear Victor, gives me more pleasure than I have for some time experienced. If you feel thus, we shall assuredly be happy, however present events may cast a gloom over us.

"We have been unfortunate, and recent events have drawn us from that every-day tranquillity befitting my years and infirmities. You are younger; yet I do not suppose, possessed as you are of a competent fortune, that an early marriage would at all interfere with any future plans of honour and utility that you may have formed.

"Do not suppose, however, that I wish to dictate happiness to you. Interpret my words with candour and answer me, I conjure you, with confidence and sincerity."

I revolved rapidly in my mind a multitude of thoughts, and
endeavoured to arrive at some conclusion. Alas! to me the idea of
an immediate union with my cousin was one of horror and dismay.
I was bound by a solemn promise, which I had not yet fulfilled, and
dared not break. I must perform my engagement, and let the monster
depart with his mate, before I allowed myself to enjoy the delight of
an union from which I expected peace.

I remembered the necessity of journeying to England to those
philosophers of that country, whose knowledge and discoveries were
of indispensable use to me in my present undertaking.

Our plan was soon arranged. I should travel to Strasburgh, where
Clerval would join me. It was agreed that the tour should occupy the
space of two years.

My union with Elizabeth should take place immediately on my
return to Geneva.

"These two years will pass swiftly, and it
will be the last delay that will oppose itself
to your happiness. And, indeed, I earnestly
desire that period to arrive, when
we shall all be united, and
neither hopes or fears arise to
disturb our domestic calm."

It was in the latter end of August that I departed. Elizabeth approved of the reasons of my departure, and only regretted that she had not the same opportunities. She wept as she bade me farewell, and entreated me to return happy and tranquil.

"We all depend upon you."

I threw myself into the carriage that was to convey me away. I remembered only to order that my chemical instruments should be packed to go with me: for I resolved to fulfil my promise while abroad, and return, if possible, a free man. Filled with dreary imaginations, my eyes were fixed and unobserving.

After some days spent in listless indolence I arrived at Strasburgh, where I waited two days for Clerval.

126

Alas, how great was the contrast between us! He was alive to every new scene; joyful when he saw the beauties of the setting sun, and more happy when he beheld it rise.

"This is what it is to live; now I enjoy existence!

"But you, my dear Frankenstein, wherefore are you desponding and sorrowful?"

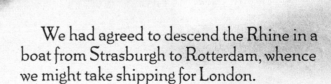

In truth, I was occupied by gloomy thoughts, and neither saw the descent of the evening star, nor the golden sun-rise reflected in the Rhine.

We had agreed to descend the Rhine in a boat from Strasburgh to Rotterdam, whence we might take shipping for London.

Even I, depressed in mind, and my spirits continually agitated by gloomy feelings, was pleased.

I lay at the bottom of the boat, and, as I gazed on the cloudless blue sky, I seemed to drink in a tranquillity to which I had long been a stranger. And if these were my sensations, who can describe those of Henry? He felt as if he had been transported to Fairyland, and enjoyed a happiness seldom tasted by man.

"I have seen the most beautiful scenes of my own country; but this country, Victor, pleases me more than all those wonders."

Clerval! beloved friend! He was a being
formed in the "very poetry of nature." His wild
and enthusiastic imagination was chastened by
the sensibility of his heart. His soul overflowed
with ardent affections, and his friendship was of
that devoted and wondrous nature that the worldly-
minded teach us to look for only in the imagination.
And where does he now exist? Is this gentle and
lovely being lost for ever? Has this mind so replete
with ideas, which formed a world, whose existence
depended on the life of its creator; has this mind
perished? Does it now only exist in my memory?
No, it is not thus; your form so divinely wrought,
and beaming with beauty, has decayed, but your
spirit still visits and consoles your unhappy friend.
  At length we saw the numerous steeples of
London, St. Paul's towering above all, and the
Tower famed in English history.

London was our present point of rest; we determined to remain several months in this wonderful and celebrated city.

I was principally occupied with the means of obtaining the information necessary for the completion of my promise, and quickly availed myself of the letters of introduction that I had brought with me, addressed to the most distinguished natural philosophers.

I saw an insurmountable barrier placed between me and my fellow-men; this barrier was sealed with the blood of William and Justine; and to reflect on the events connected with those names filled my soul with anguish.

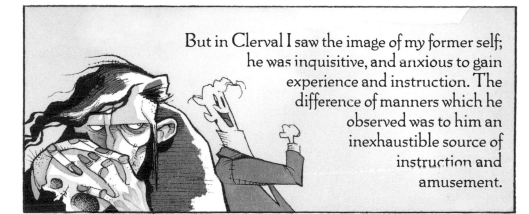

But in Clerval I saw the image of my former self; he was inquisitive, and anxious to gain experience and instruction. The difference of manners which he observed was to him an inexhaustible source of instruction and amusement.

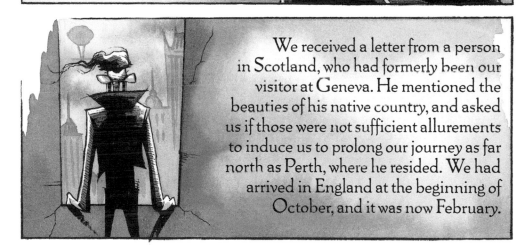

I often refused to accompany him, alleging another engagement, that I might remain alone. I now also began to collect the materials necessary for my new creation.

We received a letter from a person in Scotland, who had formerly been our visitor at Geneva. He mentioned the beauties of his native country, and asked us if those were not sufficient allurements to induce us to prolong our journey as far north as Perth, where he resided. We had arrived in England at the beginning of October, and it was now February.

We accordingly determined to commence our journey towards the north at the expiration of another month. I packed my chemical instruments, and the materials I had collected, resolving to finish my labours in some obscure nook in the northern highlands of Scotland.

I enjoyed this scene; and yet my enjoyment was embittered. During my youthful days discontent never visited my mind; and if I was ever overcome by ennui, the sight of what is beautiful in nature, or the study of what is excellent and sublime in the productions of man, could always interest my heart, and communicate elasticity to my spirits.

But I am a blasted tree; the bolt has entered my soul; and I felt then that I should survive to exhibit what I shall soon cease to be—a miserable spectacle of wrecked humanity, pitiable to others, and abhorrent to myself.

I had now neglected my promise for some time, and I feared the effects of the daemon's disappointment. He might remain in Switzerland, and wreak his vengeance on my relatives. Sometimes I thought that the fiend followed me, and might expedite my remissness by murdering my companion. When these thoughts possessed me, I would not quit Henry for a moment, but followed him as his shadow, to protect him from the fancied rage of his destroyer. I had indeed drawn down a horrible curse upon my head, as mortal as that of crime.

We passed through Coupar, St. Andrews, and along the banks of the Tay, to Perth, where our friend expected us. But I was in no mood to laugh and talk with strangers, or enter into their feelings or plans with the good humour expected from a guest; and accordingly I told Clerval that I wished to make the tour of Scotland alone.

"I may be absent a month or two; but do not interfere with my motions, I entreat you: leave me to peace and solitude for a short time; and when I return, I hope it will be with a lighter heart, more congenial to your own temper."

With this resolution I traversed the northern highlands, and fixed on one of the remotest of the Orkneys as the scene of my labours.

It was a place fitted for such a work, being hardly more than a rock, whose high sides were continually beaten upon by the waves.

On the whole island there were but three miserable huts, and one of these was vacant when I arrived. This I hired. It contained but two rooms. The thatch had fallen in, the walls were unplastered, and the door was off its hinges.

As I proceeded in my labour, it became every day more horrible to me.

Sometimes I could not prevail on myself to enter my laboratory for several days; and at other times I toiled day and night in order to complete my work. It was indeed a filthy process in which I was engaged. I went to it in cold blood, and my heart often sickened at the work of my hands.

I worked on, and my labour was already considerably advanced. I looked towards its completion with a tremulous and eager hope.

CHAPTER THREE

I sat one evening in my laboratory; the sun had set, and the moon was just rising from the sea; I had not sufficient light for my employment, and I remained idle, in a pause of consideration of whether I should leave my labour for the night, or hasten its conclusion by an unremitting attention to it.

Three years before I was engaged in the same manner, and had created a fiend whose unparalleled barbarity had desolated my heart, and filled it for ever with the bitterest remorse.

I was now about to form another being, of whose dispositions I was alike ignorant; she might become ten thousand times more malignant than her mate, and delight, for its own sake, in murder and wretchedness. He had sworn to quit the neighbourhood of man, and hide himself in deserts; but she had not; and she, who in all probability was to become a thinking and reasoning animal, might refuse to comply with a compact made before her creation. They might even hate each other; the creature who already lived loathed his own deformity, and might he not conceive a greater abhorrence for it when it came before his eyes in the female form? She also might turn with disgust from him to the superior beauty of man; she might quit him, and he be again alone, exasperated by the fresh provocation of being deserted by one of his own species.

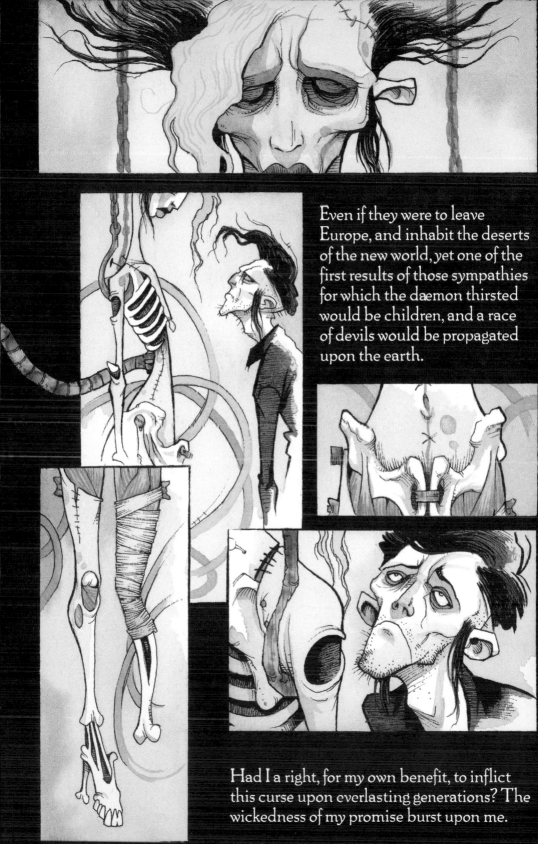

Even if they were to leave Europe, and inhabit the deserts of the new world, yet one of the first results of those sympathies for which the dæmon thirsted would be children, and a race of devils would be propagated upon the earth.

Had I a right, for my own benefit, to inflict this curse upon everlasting generations? The wickedness of my promise burst upon me.

I trembled, and my heart failed within me; when, on looking up, I saw, by the light of the moon, the dæmon at the casement. A ghastly grin wrinkled his lips as he gazed on me. Yes, he had followed me in my travels; he had loitered in forests, hid himself in caves, or taken refuge in wide and desert heaths; and he now came to mark my progress, and claim the fulfilment of my promise.

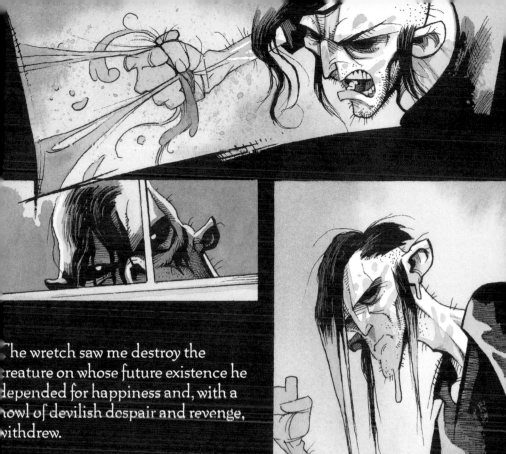

The wretch saw me destroy the creature on whose future existence he depended for happiness and, with a howl of devilish despair and revenge, withdrew.

I left the room, and, locking the door, made a solemn vow in my own heart never to resume my labours.

Several hours passed, and I remained near my window gazing on the sea; it was almost motionless, for the winds were hushed, and all nature reposed under the eye of the quiet moon. I felt the silence, although I was hardly conscious of its extreme profundity, until my ear was suddenly arrested by the paddling of oars near the shore, and a person landed close to my house.

In a few minutes after, I heard the creaking of my door, as if some one endeavoured to open it softly. I trembled from head to foot; I was overcome by the sensation of helplessness, so often felt in frightful dreams, when you in vain endeavour to fly from an impending danger, and was rooted to the spot.

Presently I heard the sound of footsteps along the passage; the door opened, and the wretch whom I dreaded appeared. Shutting the door, he approached me, and said, in a smothered voice—

"You have destroyed the work which you began; what is it that you intend?

"*Do you dare to break your promise? I have endured toil and misery, incalculable fatigue, and cold, and hunger; do you dare destroy my hopes?*"

"*Begone! I do break my promise; never will I create another like yourself, equal in deformity and wickedness.*"

"*You believe yourself miserable, but I can make you so wretched that the light of day will be hateful to you. You are my creator, but I am your master—obey!*"

"*The hour of my weakness is past, and the period of your power is arrived. Your threats cannot move me to do an act of wickedness. Shall I, in cool blood, set loose upon the earth a dæmon, whose delight is in death and wretchedness. Begone!*"

"*Your hours will pass in dread and misery, and soon the bolt will fall which must ravish from you your happiness for ever. Are you to be happy, while I grovel in the intensity of my wretchedness? Beware; for I am fearless. You shall repent of the injuries you inflict.*"

"I go; but I shall be with you on your wedding-night."

All was again silent; but his words rung in my ears. Why had I not followed him, and closed with him in mortal strife? I shuddered to think who might be the next victim sacrificed to his insatiate revenge.

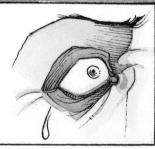

And then I thought again of his words—"I shall be with you on your wedding-night." In that hour I should die, and at once satisfy and extinguish his malice.

The next morning, at day-break, I summoned sufficient courage, and unlocked the door of my laboratory. The remains of the half-finished creature I had destroyed lay scattered on the floor, and I almost felt as if I had mangled the living flesh of a human being. With trembling hand I conveyed the instruments out of the room; but I reflected that I ought not to leave the relics of my work to excite the horror and suspicion of the peasants, and I accordingly put them into a basket, with a great quantity of stones, and laying them up, determined to throw them into the sea that very night.

Between two and three in the morning the moon rose; and I then, putting my basket aboard a little skiff, sailed out about four miles from the shore. The scene was perfectly solitary. I took advantage of the darkness, and cast my basket into the sea.

I listened to the gurgling sound as it sunk, and stretched myself at the bottom of the boat. I heard the sound of the boat, as its keel cut through the waves; the murmur lulled me, and in a short time I slept soundly.

I do not know how long I remained in this situation, but when I awoke I found that the sun had already mounted considerably. The waves continually threatened the safety of my little skiff. I found that the wind must have driven me far from the coast from which I had embarked.

I had already been out many hours, and felt the torment of a burning thirst, a prelude to my other sufferings. I looked upon the sea, it was to be my grave.

"Fiend, your task is already fulfilled!"

Some hours passed thus; but by degrees, as the sun declined towards the horizon, the wind died away into a gentle breeze, and the sea became free from breakers. But these gave place to a heavy swell; I felt sick, and hardly able to hold the rudder, when suddenly I saw a line of high land towards the south.

How mutable are our feelings, and how strange is that clinging love we have of life even in the excess of misery!

I easily perceived the traces of cultivation and found myself suddenly transported back to the neighbourhood of civilized man.

As I was occupied in fixing the boat, several people crowded towards the spot. They seemed very much surprised at my appearance; but, instead of offering me any assistance, whispered together with gestures that at any other time might have produced in me a slight sensation of alarm.

"My good friends, will you be so kind as to tell me the name of this town, and inform me where I am?"

"You will know that soon enough. Maybe you are come to a place that will not prove much to your taste; but you will not be consulted as to your quarters, I promise you."

"Why do you answer me so roughly? Surely it is not the custom of Englishmen to receive strangers so inhospitably."

"I do not know what the custom of the English may be; but it is the custom of the Irish to hate villains."

"Come, Sir, you must follow me to Mr. Kirwin's, to give an account of yourself."

"Who is Mr. Kirwin?"

"Mr. Kirwin is a magistrate; and you are to give an account of the death of a gentleman who was found murdered here last night."

This answer startled me; but I presently recovered myself. I was innocent; that could easily be proved: accordingly I followed my conductor in silence, and was led to one of the best houses in the town. Little did I then expect the calamity that was in a few moments to overwhelm me, and extinguish in horror and despair all fear of ignominy or death.

CHAPTER FOUR

I was soon introduced into the presence of the magistrate, an old benevolent man, with calm and mild manners. He looked upon me, however, with some degree of severity; and then, turning towards my conductors, he asked who appeared as witnesses on this occasion.

About half a dozen men came forward; and one being selected by the magistrate, he deposed that he had been out fishing the night before with his son and brother-in-law, Daniel Nugent. As he was proceeding along the sands, he struck his foot against something. His companions came up and, by the light of their lantern, they found the body of a man, who was to all appearance dead. Their first supposition was that it was some person who had drowned, and was thrown on shore by the waves; but, upon examination, they found that the clothes were not wet, and even that the body was not then cold. He appeared to be about five and twenty years of age. He had apparently been strangled; for there was no sign of any violence, except the black mark of fingers on his neck.

The first part of this deposition did not in the least interest me; but when the mark of the fingers was mentioned, I remembered the murder of my brother, and felt myself extremely agitated; my limbs trembled, and a mist came over my eyes, which obliged me to lean on a chair for support. The magistrate observed me with a keen eye, and of course drew an unfavourable augury from my manner.

The son confirmed his father's account: but when Daniel Nugent was called, he swore positively that he saw a boat, with a single man in it, at a short distance from the shore; and, as far as he could judge by the light of a few stars, it was the same boat in which I had just landed.

A woman deposed that about an hour before she heard of the discovery of the body, she saw a boat, with only one man in it, push off from that part of the shore where the corpse was afterwards found.

Several other men were examined concerning my landing; and they agreed, that, with the strong north wind that had arisen during the night, it was very probable that I had beaten about for many hours, and had been obliged to return nearly to the same spot from which I had departed.

Mr. Kirwin, on hearing this evidence, desired that I should be taken into the room where the body lay for interment, that it might be observed what effect the sight of it would produce upon me.

I entered the room where the corpse lay, and was led up to the coffin.

How can I describe my sensations on beholding it? The trial, the presence of the magistrate and witnesses, passed like a dream from my memory, when I saw the lifeless form of Henry Clerval stretched before me.

"Have my murderous machinations deprived you also, my dearest Henry, of life?"

The human frame could no longer support the agonizing suffering that I endured, and I was carried out of the room in strong convulsions.

A fever succeeded to this. I lay for two months on the point of death: my ravings, as I afterwards heard, were frightful; I called myself the murderer of William, of Justine, and of Clerval.

Sometimes I entreated my attendants to assist me in the destruction of the fiend by whom I was tormented; and, at others, I felt the fingers of the monster already grasping my neck, and screamed aloud with agony and terror.

Why did I not die? How many youthful lovers have been one day in the bloom of health and hope, and the next a prey for worms and the decay of the tomb! Of what materials was I made, that I could thus resist so many shocks, which, like the turning of the wheel, continually renewed the torture.

But I was doomed to live; and, in two months, found myself in a prison, stretched on a wretched bed.

The whole series of my life appeared to me as a dream; I sometimes doubted if indeed it were all true, for it never presented itself to my mind with the force of reality.

As the images that floated before me became more distinct, I grew feverish; a darkness pressed around me; no one was near me who soothed me with the gentle voice of love; no dear hand supported me.

Who could be interested in the fate of a murderer, but the hangman who would gain his fee?

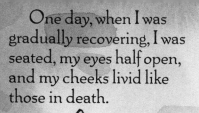

One day, when I was gradually recovering, I was seated, my eyes half open, and my cheeks livid like those in death.

I was overcome by gloom and misery. At one time I considered whether I should not declare myself guilty, and suffer the penalty of the law, less innocent than poor Justine had been.

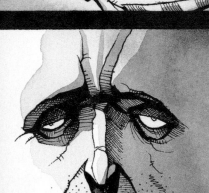

The door of my apartment was opened, and Mr. Kirwin entered. His countenance expressed sympathy and compassion; he drew a chair close to mine, and addressed me in French—

"It was not until a day or two after your illness that I thought of examining your dress, that I might discover some trace by which I could send to your relations an account of your misfortune and illness. I found several letters, and, among others, one which I discovered from its commencement to be from your father. I instantly wrote to Geneva: nearly two months have elapsed since the departure of my letter. But you are ill; even now you tremble: you are unfit for agitation of any kind."

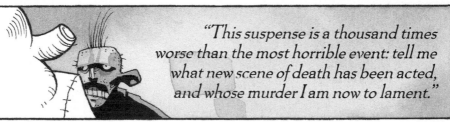

"This suspense is a thousand times worse than the most horrible event: tell me what new scene of death has been acted, and whose murder I am now to lament."

"Your family is perfectly well, and some one, a friend, is come to visit you."

I know not by what chain of thought the idea presented itself, but it instantly darted into my mind that the murderer had come to mock at my misery, and taunt me with the death of Clerval, as a new incitement for me to comply with his hellish desires. I put my hand before my eyes, and cried out in agony—

"Oh! take him away! I cannot see him; for God's sake, do not let him enter!"

Mr. Kirwin regarded me with a troubled countenance. He could not help regarding my exclamation as a presumption of my guilt, and said, in rather a severe tone—

"I should have thought, young man, that the presence of your father would have been welcome, instead of inspiring such violent repugnance."

"My father!"

Nothing, at this moment, could have given me greater pleasure than the arrival of my father. I stretched out my hand to him.

"Are you then safe—and Elizabeth?"

My father calmed me with assurances of their welfare.

"What a place is this that you inhabit, my son! You travelled to seek happiness, but a fatality seems to pursue you. And poor Clerval—"

"Alas! yes, my father, some destiny of the most horrible kind hangs over me, and I must live to fulfil it."

The appearance of my father was to me like that of my good angel.

I had already been three months in prison; and although I was still weak, and in continual danger of a relapse, I was obliged to travel nearly a hundred miles to the county-town, where the court was held.

I saw around me nothing but a dense and frightful darkness, penetrated by no light but the glimmer of two eyes that glared upon me.

Sometimes they were the expressive eyes of Henry, languishing in death, the dark orbs nearly covered by the lids, and the long black lashes that fringed them; sometimes it was the watery clouded eyes of the monster, as I first saw them in my chamber at Ingolstadt.

The grand jury rejected the bill, on its being proved that I was on the Orkney Islands at the hour the body of my friend was found, and a fortnight after my removal I was liberated from prison and allowed to return to my native country.

"He may be innocent of the murder, but he has certainly a bad conscience."

We had resolved not to go to London. I dreaded to see again those places in which I had enjoyed a few moments of tranquillity with my beloved Clerval. As for my father, his desires and exertions were bounded to again seeing me restored to health and peace of mind. My grief and gloom was obstinate, but he would not despair.

"Alas! my father, how little do you know me. Justine, poor unhappy Justine, was as innocent as I, and she suffered the same charge; she died for it; and I am the cause of this—I murdered her. William, Justine, and Henry—they all died by my hands."

"What do you mean, Victor? are you mad? My dear son, I entreat you never to make such an assertion again."

"I am not mad. I am the assassin of those most innocent victims; they died by my machinations."

The conclusion of this speech convinced my father that my ideas were deranged, and he instantly changed the subject of our conversation.

As time passed away I became more calm: misery had her dwelling in my heart, but I no longer talked in the same incoherent manner of my own crimes. I curbed the imperious voice of wretchedness, which sometimes desired to declare itself to the whole world.

We arrived at Paris.

In this city, I received the following letter from Elizabeth—

My Dearest Friend,

It gave me the greatest pleasure to receive a letter from my uncle dated at Paris; you are no longer at a formidable distance, and I may hope to see you in less than a fortnight. My poor cousin, how much you must have suffered! I would not disturb you at this period, when so many misfortunes weigh upon you; but a conversation that I had with my uncle previous to his departure renders some explanation necessary before we meet.

You well know, Victor, that our union had been the favourite plan of your parents ever since our infancy. We were affectionate playfellows during childhood. But as brother and sister often entertain a lively affection towards each other, without desiring a more intimate union, may not such also be our case? Tell me, dearest Victor. Do you not love another?

You have travelled; you have spent several years of your life at Ingolstadt; and I confess to you, my friend, that when I saw you last autumn so unhappy, flying to solitude, from the society of every creature, I could not help supposing that you might regret our connexion, and believe yourself bound in honour to fulfil the wishes of your parents. I confess to you, my cousin, that I love you, and that in my airy dreams of futurity you have been my constant friend and companion. But it is your happiness I desire as well as my own when I declare to you that our marriage would render me eternally miserable, unless it were the dictate of your own free choice. Ah, Victor, be assured that your cousin and playmate has too sincere a love for you not to be made miserable by this supposition. Be happy, my friend; and if you obey me in this one request, remain satisfied that nothing on earth will have the power to interrupt my tranquillity.

Do not let this letter disturb you; do not answer it to-morrow, or the next day, or even until you come, if it will give you pain. My uncle will send me news of your health; and if I see but one smile on your lips when we meet, occasioned by this or any other exertion of mine, I shall need no other happiness.

Elizabeth Lavenza.

Geneva, May 18th.

This letter revived in my memory what I had before forgotten, the threat of the fiend—"I will be with you on your wedding-night!" On that night would the daemon employ every art to destroy me, and tear me from the glimpse of happiness which promised partly to console my sufferings. On that night he had determined to consummate his crimes by my death. If the monster executed his threat, death was inevitable; yet, again, I considered whether my marriage would hasten my fate. My destruction might indeed arrive a few months sooner; but if my torturer should suspect that I postponed it, influenced by his menaces, he would surely find other, and perhaps more dreadful, means of revenge. I resolved, therefore, that if my immediate union with my cousin would conduce either to her's or my father's happiness, my adversary's designs against my life should not retard it a single hour.

I fear, my beloved girl, little happiness remains for us on earth; yet all that I may one day enjoy is concentered in you. Chase away your idle fears; to you alone do I consecrate my life, and my endeavours for contentment. I have one secret, Elizabeth, a dreadful one; when revealed to you, it will chill your frame with horror, and then, far from being surprised at my misery, you will only wonder that I survive what I have endured. I will confide this tale of misery and terror to you the day after our marriage shall take place; for, my sweet cousin, there must be perfect confidence between us. But until then, I conjure you, do not mention or allude to it. This I most earnestly entreat, and I know you will comply.

Victor Frankenstein

We returned to Geneva. My cousin
welcomed me with warm affection;
yet tears were in her eyes.

She was thinner, and had lost much
of that heavenly vivacity that had before
charmed me; but her gentleness, and
soft looks of compassion, made her a
more fit companion for one blasted and
miserable as I was.

Elizabeth alone had the power to soothe me
when transported by passion, and inspire me with
human feelings when sunk in torpor. She wept
with me, and for me. When reason returned,
she would remonstrate, and endeavour to
inspire me with resignation. Ah! it is well
for the unfortunate to be resigned, but
for the guilty there is no peace.

Soon after my arrival
my father spoke of my
immediate marriage
with my cousin.

"Heavy misfortunes have befallen us; but let us only cling closer to what remains, and transfer our love for those whom we have lost to those who yet live. Our circle will be small, but bound close by the ties of affection and mutual misfortune."

I agreed with my father, that if my cousin would consent, the ceremony should take place in ten days, and thus put, as I imagined, the seal to my fate. "I shall be with you on your wedding-night."

As the period fixed for our marriage drew nearer, whether from cowardice or a prophetic feeling, I felt my heart sink within me. But I concealed my feelings by an appearance of hilarity, that brought smiles and joy to the countenance of my father, but hardly deceived the ever-watchful and nicer eye of Elizabeth.

I shut up, as well as I could, in my own heart the anxiety that preyed there, and entered with seeming earnestness into the plans of my father, although they might only serve as the decorations of my tragedy. In the mean time I took every precaution to defend my person, in case the fiend should openly attack me. I carried pistols and a dagger constantly about me, and was ever on the watch to prevent artifice. As the period approached, the threat appeared more as a delusion, while the happiness I hoped for in my marriage wore a greater appearance of certainty.

After the ceremony was performed, a large party assembled at my father's, it was agreed that Elizabeth and I should pass the afternoon and night at Evian, and return the next morning.

Those were the last moments of my life during which I enjoyed the feeling of happiness. We enjoyed the beauty of the scene, sometimes on one side of the lake, where we saw Mont Salêve, the pleasant banks of the Montalêgre, and at a distance, surmounting all, the beautiful Mont Blânc, and the assemblage of mountains that in vain endeavor to emulate her; sometimes coasting the opposite banks, we saw the mighty Jura opposing its dark side to the ambition that would quit its native country.

"You are sorrowful, my love. Ah! if you knew what I have suffered, and what I may yet endure, you would endeavour to let me taste the quiet, and freedom from despair, that this one day at least permits me to enjoy."

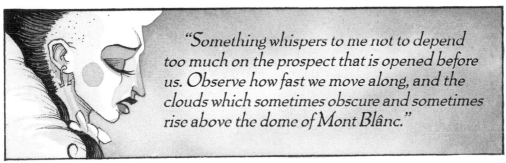

"Something whispers to me not to depend too much on the prospect that is opened before us. Observe how fast we move along, and the clouds which sometimes obscure and sometimes rise above the dome of Mont Blânc."

The Alps here come closer to the lake, and we approached the amphitheatre of mountains which forms its eastern boundary. The sun sunk beneath the horizon as we landed; and as I touched the shore, I felt those cares and fears revive, which soon were to clasp me, and cling to me for ever.

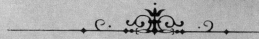

CHAPTER SIX

The wind, which had fallen in the south, now rose with great violence in the west. The moon had reached her summit in the heavens, and was beginning to descend; the clouds swept across it swifter than the flight of the vulture, and dimmed her rays, while the lake reflected the scene of the busy heavens, rendered still busier by the restless waves that were beginning to rise. Suddenly a heavy storm of rain descended.

I had been calm during the day; but so soon as night obscured the shapes of objects, a thousand fears arose in my mind. I was anxious and watchful, while my right hand grasped a pistol which was hidden in my bosom; every sound terrified me.

"What is it that agitates you, my dear Victor? What is it you fear?"

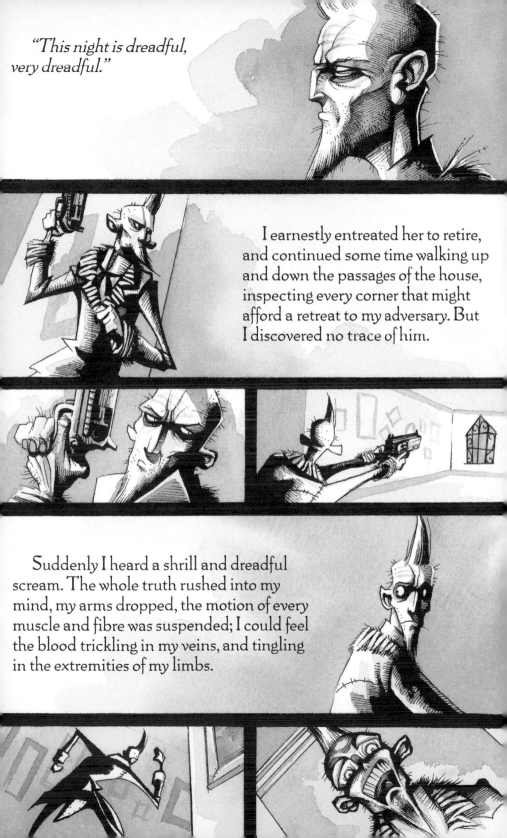

"This night is dreadful, very dreadful."

I earnestly entreated her to retire, and continued some time walking up and down the passages of the house, inspecting every corner that might afford a retreat to my adversary. But I discovered no trace of him.

Suddenly I heard a shrill and dreadful scream. The whole truth rushed into my mind, my arms dropped, the motion of every muscle and fibre was suspended; I could feel the blood trickling in my veins, and tingling in the extremities of my limbs.

A fiend had snatched from me every hope of future happiness:
no creature had ever been so miserable as I was.

But why should I dwell upon the incidents that followed this
last overwhelming event. Mine has been a tale of horrors.

Know that, one by one, my friends were snatched away; I was left
desolate. My own strength is exhausted; and I must tell, in a few
words, what remains of my hideous narration.

My father yet lived; but sunk under the tidings that I bore. I see him now, his eyes wandered in vacancy. Cursed, cursed be the fiend that doomed him to waste in wretchedness!

He could not live under the horrors that were accumulated around him; an apoplectic fit was brought on, and in a few days he died in my arms.

What then became of me? Chains and darkness were the only objects that pressed upon me. Melancholy followed, but by degrees I gained a clear conception of my miseries and situation, and was then released from my prison. For they had called me mad; and during many months, as I understood, a solitary cell had been my habitation.

As the memory of past misfortunes pressed upon me, I began to reflect on their cause—the monster whom I had created, the miserable dæmon whom I had sent abroad into the world for my destruction. I was possessed by a maddening rage when I thought of him, and desired and ardently prayed that I might have him within my grasp to wreak a great and signal revenge on his cursed head.

CHAPTER SEVEN

My present situation was one in which all voluntary thought was swallowed up and lost. I was hurried away by fury; revenge alone endowed me with strength and composure; it modelled my feelings, and allowed me to be calculating and calm, at periods when otherwise delirium or death would have been my portion.

My first resolution was to quit Geneva for ever; my country, which, when I was happy and beloved, was dear to me, now, in my adversity, became hateful.

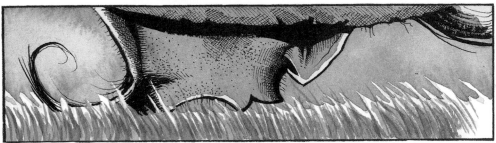

"By the sacred earth on which I kneel, by the shades that wander near me, by the deep and eternal grief that I feel, I swear; and by thee, O Night, and by the spirits that preside over thee, I swear to pursue the dæmon, who caused this misery, until he or I shall perish in mortal conflict. I call on you, spirits of the dead; and on you, wandering ministers of vengeance, to aid and conduct me in my work. Let the cursed and hellish monster drink deep of agony; let him feel the despair that now torments me."

I was answered through the stillness of night by a loud and fiendish laugh. It rung on my ears long and heavily; the mountains re-echoed it, and I felt as if all hell surrounded me with mockery and laughter.

"I am satisfied: miserable wretch! You have determined to live, and I am satisfied."

I darted towards the spot from which the sound proceeded; but the devil eluded my grasp. Suddenly the broad disk of the moon arose, and shone full upon his ghastly and distorted shape, as he fled with more than mortal speed.

And now my wanderings began, which are to cease but with life.

I have traversed a vast portion of the earth, and have endured all the hardships which travellers, in deserts and barbarous countries, are wont to meet.

How I have lived I hardly know; many times have I stretched my failing limbs upon the sandy plain, and prayed for death.

But revenge kept me alive; I dared not die, and leave my adversary in being.

I was cursed by some devil, and carried about with me my eternal hell.

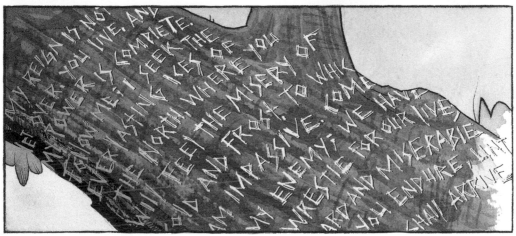

Scoffing devil! Again do I vow vengeance; again do I devote thee, miserable fiend, to torture and death. Never will I omit my search, until he or I perish; and then with what ecstacy shall I join my Elizabeth, and those who even now prepare for me the reward of my tedious toil and horrible pilgrimage.

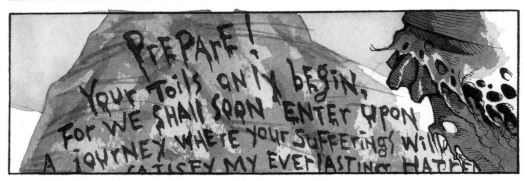

PrEPArE!
Your Toils only begin,
For WE SHall SooN ENTEr upoN
A JouRNEY WHEre Your SuFFeriNgs will
SATISFY MY EVErlASTiNG HATrEd

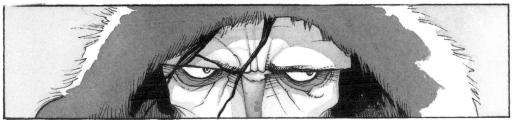

Oh! with what a burning gush did hope revisit my heart! Warm tears filled my eyes, which I hastily wiped away, that they might not intercept the view I had of the dæmon; but still my sight was dimmed by the burning drops, until, giving way to the emotions that oppressed me, I wept aloud.

But now, when I appeared almost within grasp of my enemy, my hopes were suddenly extinguished, and I lost all trace of him more utterly than I had ever done before. A ground sea was heard; the thunder of its progress, as the waters rolled and swelled beneath me, became every moment more ominous and terrific. The sea roared; and, as with the mighty shock of an earthquake, it split, and cracked with a tremendous and overwhelming sound.

In this manner many appalling hours passed; several of my dogs died; and I myself was about to sink under the accumulation of distress, when I saw your vessel riding at anchor, and holding forth to me hopes of succour and life.

I had no conception that vessels ever came so far north, and was astounded at the sight. I quickly destroyed part of my sledge to construct oars; and by these means was enabled, with infinite fatigue, to move my ice-raft in the direction of your ship. I had determined, if you were going southward, still to trust myself to the mercy of the seas, rather than abandon my purpose. I hoped to induce you to grant me a boat with which I could still pursue my enemy. But your direction was northward. You took me on board when my vigour was exhausted, and I should soon have sunk under my multiplied hardships into a death, which I still dread—for my task is unfulfilled.

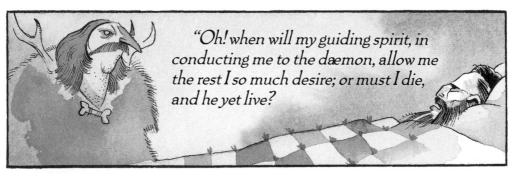

"Oh! when will my guiding spirit, in conducting me to the dæmon, allow me the rest I so much desire; or must I die, and he yet live?

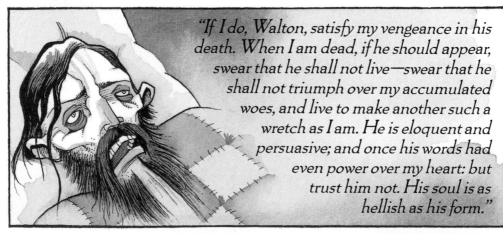

"If I do, Walton, satisfy my vengeance in his death. When I am dead, if he should appear, swear that he shall not live—swear that he shall not triumph over my accumulated woes, and live to make another such a wretch as I am. He is eloquent and persuasive; and once his words had even power over my heart: but trust him not. His soul is as hellish as his form."

August 26th.

You have read this strange and terrific story, Margaret; and do you not feel your blood congealed with horror, like that which even now curdles mine? His tale is connected, and told with an appearance of the simplest truth. Such a monster has then existence; I cannot doubt it; yet I am lost in surprise and admiration. Sometimes I endeavoured to gain from Frankenstein the particulars of his creature's formation; but on this point he was impenetrable.

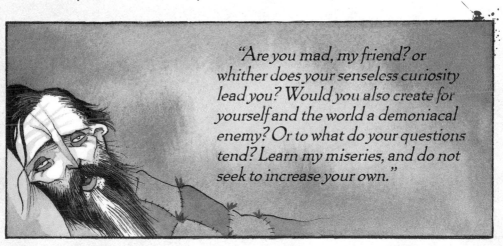

"Are you mad, my friend? or whither does your senseless curiosity lead you? Would you also create for yourself and the world a demoniacal enemy? Or to what do your questions tend? Learn my miseries, and do not seek to increase your own."

Thus has a week passed away, while I have listened to the strangest tale that ever imagination formed. I wish to soothe him; yet can I counsel one so infinitely miserable, so destitute of every hope of consolation, to live? Yet he enjoys one comfort, the offspring of solitude and delirium: he believes, that, when in dreams he holds converse with his friends, and derives from that communion consolation for his miseries, or excitements to his vengeance, that they are not the creations of his fancy, but the real beings who visit him from the regions of a remote world.

ur conversations are not always confined to his own history and misfortunes. On every point of general literature he displays unbounded knowledge, and a quick and piercing apprehension. His eloquence is forcible and touching. What a glorious creature must he have been in the days of his prosperity, when he is thus noble and godlike in ruin. He seems to feel his own worth, and the greatness of his fall.

Must I then lose this admirable being? I have longed for a friend; I have sought one who would sympathize with and love me. Behold, on these desert seas I have found such a one; but, I fear, I have gained him only to know his value, and lose him.

"When younger, I felt as if I were destined for some great enterprise. This feeling, which supported me in the commencement of my career, now serves only to plunge me lower in the dust. All my speculations and hopes are as nothing; and, like the archangel who aspired to omnipotence, I am chained in an eternal hell. Oh! my friend, if you had known me as I once was, you would not recognize me in this state of degradation.

"Wherever I am, the soothing voice of my Elizabeth, and the conversation of Clerval will be ever whispered in my ear. They are dead; and but one feeling in such a solitude can persuade me to preserve my life. If I were engaged in any high undertaking or design, fraught with extensive utility to my fellow-creatures, then could I live to fulfil it. But such is not my destiny; I must pursue and destroy the being to whom I gave existence; then my lot on earth will be fulfilled, and I may die."

September 2nd.

My Beloved Sister; I write to you, encompassed by peril, and ignorant whether I am ever doomed to see again dear England, and the dearer friends that inhabit it. I am surrounded by mountains of ice, which admit of no escape, and threaten every moment to crush my vessel. The brave fellows, whom I have persuaded to be my companions, look towards me for aid; but I have none to bestow.

Yet what, Margaret, will be the state of your mind? You will not hear of my destruction, and you will anxiously await my return. Years will pass, and you will have visitings of despair, and yet be tortured by hope. Oh! my beloved sister, the sickening failings of your heart-felt expectations are, in prospect, more terrible to me than my own death. But you have a husband, and lovely children; you may be happy: heaven bless you, and make you so!

My unfortunate guest regards me with the tenderest compassion. He endeavours to fill me with hope; and talks as if life were a possession which he valued. Even the sailors feel the power of his eloquence: when he speaks, they no longer despair; he rouses their energies, and, while they hear his voice, they believe these vast mountains of ice are mole-hills, which will vanish before the resolutions of man. These feelings are transitory; each day's expectation delayed fills them with fear, and I almost dread a mutiny caused by this despair.

Deptember 5th.

We are still surrounded by mountains of ice, still in imminent danger of being crushed in their conflict. The cold is excessive, and many of my unfortunate comrades have already found a grave amidst this scene of desolation. Frankenstein has daily declined in health: a feverish fire still glimmers in his eyes; but he is exhausted, and, when suddenly roused to any exertion, he speedily sinks again into apparent lifelessness.

I mentioned in my last letter the fears I entertained of a mutiny. This morning, I was roused by half a dozen of the sailors, who desired admission into the cabin. Their leader told me that he and his companions had been chosen by the other sailors to come in deputation to me, to make me a demand, which, in justice, I could not refuse. We were immured in ice, and should probably never escape; but if the ice should dissipate, and a free passage be opened, they desired that I should engage with a solemn promise, that I would instantly direct my course southward.

This speech troubled me. I had not despaired; nor had I yet conceived the idea of returning, if set free. Yet could I, in justice, or even in possibility, refuse this demand? I hesitated before I answered; when Frankenstein roused himself; his eyes sparkled, and his cheeks flushed with momentary vigour.

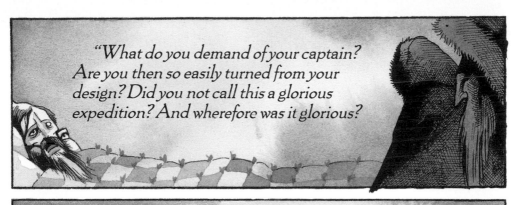

"What do you demand of your captain? Are you then so easily turned from your design? Did you not call this a glorious expedition? And wherefore was it glorious?

"Not because the way was smooth and placid as a southern sea, but because it was full of dangers and terror; because, at every new incident, your fortitude was to be called forth, and your courage exhibited; because danger and death surrounded, and these dangers you were to brave and overcome.

"For this was it a glorious, an honourable undertaking. You were hereafter to be hailed as the benefactors of your species; your name adored, as belonging to brave men who encountered death for honour and the benefit of mankind. And now, you are content to be handed down as men who had not strength enough to endure cold and peril. Oh! be men, or be more than men. This ice is not made of such stuff as your hearts might be. Do not return to your families with the stigma of disgrace marked on your brows. Return as heroes who have fought and conquered, and who know not what it is to turn their backs on the foe."

They retired, and I turned towards my friend; but he was sunk in languor, and almost deprived of life.

September 12th.

It is past; I am returning to England. I have lost my hopes of utility and glory;—I have lost my friend. But I will endeavour to detail these bitter circumstances to you, my dear sister; and, while I am wafted towards England, and towards you, I will not despond.

September 9th, the ice began to move, and roarings like thunder were heard at a distance, as the islands split and cracked in every direction. We were in the most imminent peril; but, as we could only remain passive, my chief attention was occupied by my unfortunate guest, whose illness increased in such a degree, that he was entirely confined to his bed. The ice cracked behind us, and was driven with force towards the north; a breeze sprung from the west, and on the 11th the passage towards the south became perfectly free. When the sailors saw this, and that their return to their native country was apparently assured, a shout of tumultuous joy broke from them, loud and long-continued. Frankenstein, who was dozing, awoke, and asked the cause of the tumult.

"They shout because they will soon return to England."

"Do you then really return?"

"Alas! yes; I cannot withstand their demands. I cannot lead them unwillingly to danger, and I must return."

"Do so, if you will; but I will not. You may give up your purpose; but mine is assigned to me by heaven, surely the spirits who assist my vengeance will endow me with sufficient strength."

Saying this, he endeavoured to spring from the bed, but the exertion was too great for him; he fell back, and fainted. It was long before he was restored; and I often thought that life was entirely extinct. At length he opened his eyes, but he breathed with difficulty, and was unable to speak. The surgeon gave him a composing draught, and ordered us to leave him undisturbed. In the mean time he told me that my friend had certainly not many hours to live.

His sentence was pronounced; and I could only grieve, and be patient. Presently he called to me in a feeble voice.

"Alas! the strength I relied on is gone; I feel that I shall soon die, and he, my enemy and persecutor, may still be in being. In a fit of enthusiastic madness I created a rational creature, and was bound towards him. The task of his destruction was mine, but I have failed. When actuated by selfish and vicious motives, I asked you to undertake my unfinished work.

"Yet I cannot ask you to renounce your country and friends, and now, that you are returning to England, you will have little chance of meeting with him. I dare not ask you to do what I think right, for I may still be misled by passion.

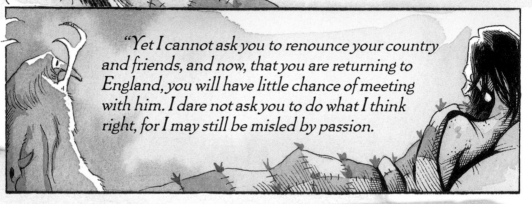

"That he should live to be an instrument of mischief disturbs me; in other respects this hour, when I momentarily expect my release, is the only happy one which I have enjoyed for several years. The forms of the beloved dead flit before me, and I hasten to their arms. Farewell, Walton! Seek happiness in tranquillity, and avoid ambition, even if it be only the apparently innocent one of distinguishing yourself in science and discoveries. Yet why do I say this? I have myself been blasted in these hopes, yet another may succeed."

His voice became fainter as he spoke; and at length, exhausted by his effort, he sunk into silence. He pressed my hand feebly, and his eyes closed for ever, while the irradiation of a gentle smile passed away from his lips.

Margaret, what comment can I make on the untimely extinction of this glorious spirit? What can I say, that will enable you to understand the depth of my sorrow? All that I should express would be inadequate and feeble. My tears flow; my mind is overshadowed by a cloud of disappointment. But I journey towards England, and I may there find consolation.

Good night, my sister.

"Oh, Frankenstein! generous and self-devoted being! what does it avail that I now ask thee to pardon me? I, who irretrievably destroyed thee by destroying all thou lovedst."

"Monster, your repentance is now superfluous. If you had listened to the voice of conscience, and heeded the stings of remorse, before you had urged your diabolical vengeance to this extremity, Frankenstein would yet have lived."

"Do you think that I was then dead to agony and remorse? Think ye that the groans of Clerval were music to my ears? My heart was fashioned to be susceptible of love and sympathy; and, when wrenched by misery to vice and hatred, it did not endure the violence of the change without torture, such as you cannot even imagine.

"I pitied Frankenstein; my pity amounted to horror: I abhorred myself. But when I discovered that he, the author of my existence, sought his own enjoyment in feelings and passions from the indulgence of which I was for ever barred, then impotent envy and bitter indignation filled me with an insatiable thirst for vengeance.

"Evil thenceforth became my good.
Urged thus far, I had no choice but to
adapt my nature to an element which
I had willingly chosen. And now it is
ended; there is my last victim."

"Wretch! It is well that you come
here to whine over the desolation that
you have made. You throw a torch into
a pile of buildings, and when they are
consumed you sit among the ruins, and
lament the fall. It is not pity that you feel;
you lament only because the
victim of your malignity is
withdrawn from your power."

"Oh, it is not thus—not thus, yet such must
be the impression conveyed to you by what
appears to be the purport of my actions.
No sympathy may I ever find. When I
first sought it, it was the love of virtue, the
feelings of happiness and affection with
which my whole being overflowed, that
I wished to be participated."

"But now, that virtue has become to me a shadow, and that happiness and affection are turned into bitter and loathing despair, in what should I seek for sympathy? I am content to suffer alone, while my sufferings shall endure.

"Once I falsely hoped to meet with beings, who, pardoning my outward form, would love me for the excellent qualities which I was capable of bringing forth. But now vice has degraded me beneath the meanest animal. The fallen angel becomes a malignant devil. Yet even that enemy of God and man had friends and associates in his desolation; I am quite alone.

"It is true that I am a wretch. I have murdered the lovely and the helpless; I have strangled the innocent as they slept, and grasped to death his throat who never injured me or any other living thing. I have devoted my creator to misery; I have pursued him even to that irremediable ruin. Here he lies, white and cold in death. I look on the hands which executed the deed; I think on the heart in which the imagination of it was conceived. Fear not that I shall be the instrument of future mischief. My work is nearly complete.

"I shall quit your vessel on the ice-raft which brought me hither, and shall seek the most northern extremity of the globe; I shall collect my funeral pile, and consume to ashes this miserable frame, that its remains may afford no light to any curious and unhallowed wretch, who would create such another as I have been. I shall die.

"He is dead who called me into being; and when I shall be no more, the very remembrance of us both will speedily vanish. I shall no longer see the sun or stars, or feel the winds play on my cheeks. Light, feeling, and sense, will pass away.

"Soon these burning miseries will be extinct. I shall ascend my funeral pile triumphantly. The light of that conflagration will fade away; my ashes will be swept into the sea by the winds. My spirit will sleep in peace; or if it thinks, it will not surely think thus."

THE END

AFTERWORD

by

GRIS GRIMLY

I've always felt that all monster fans can be divided into two teams. One team relates to Dracula, and the other team relates to Frankenstein. You can like both. You can like zombies, the wolf man, or any subgenre too. But it always comes down to Team Dracula and Team Frankenstein. Dracula fans tend to be more reserved, well educated, romantic, and put together, if I may make a generalization. On the other hand, Frankenstein fans tend to be disheveled, crude, and rebellious, all while feeling misunderstood. Neither is superior. It's the difference between Cadillacs and Lincolns.

I've always been on Team Frankenstein.

As time spins away, I'm finding that I'm not the only one whose first impressions of the Frankenstein story came from the movie. I'm speaking of course of the old black-and-white film directed by James Whale (who, I might add, was quite the upstart himself). Although this adaptation is not very loyal to Mary Shelley's book, it is structurally solid, visually awe inspiring, and emotional beyond a tent revival. More important, though, it captures that feeling of being an outsider that I mentioned above. Being a little weirdo growing up in Hicksville, USA, I identified with the monster. I stumbled from social group to social group looking for acceptance but only found harsh taunts and hard knocks. In a mental reality, the monster and I became friends. A bond between two misunderstood beings was formed. Mary Shelley intended for readers to sympathize with the monster. The story of Frankenstein reflected her own personal feelings of abandonment, and perhaps nowhere is that more evident than in the monster's account of his birth and development in Volume Two. James Whale made that connection with his film as well. This emotional string is what pulled me (and other misanthropes) into the family of the wretched.

As I've matured and developed as a professional artist, however, I have found a new kinship within the pages of *Frankenstein*: that of Victor Frankenstein himself. The moral exhortation of *Frankenstein* is to value family and friends. Beware the slippery slopes of acclimating to a life of self-absorbed achievements and fame, lest one falls into the pit of fire and brimstone. This was the path I trotted. The struggles of maintaining relationships and preventing passions from becoming obsessions were made very real for me. For the first time, I saw the world through Victor Frankenstein's eyes. It was this darkness inside myself that I unleashed into my own illustrated version.

Frankenstein has been illustrated many times, in the form of novels, comics, and picture books. My favorite is Bernie Wrightson's version, originally published in 1983. The images are gothic, sentimental, and narrative, evoking the mastership of Gustave Doré. To me, this is the quintessential version of *Frankenstein* told in its truest form. I've never understood the concept of replicating perfection. So when I accepted the task to illustrate my favorite horror story, I forged my own path. I wanted to achieve something different. I wanted to set the tale in a world that could only be visited through my imagination. Dark moral lessons exist amidst a whimsical tone. There is no past, present, or future in this land that is familiar, yet far, far away. These are the raw materials that make up a fairy tale.

Putting aside the structures of realism and horror, I tackled this monster. And what a monster it turned out to be. Illustrating these two hundred pages absorbed close to four years, an ordeal that mirrored conflicts and achievements in my own life. I encountered struggles in relationships, which ended in lost loved ones and friends. I experienced betrayal and abandonment. New relationships were formed and bonds were strengthened. I met my kindred spirit, experienced new love, engagement, and marriage. More has happened in the four years I spent illustrating *Frankenstein* than all the thirty-three years previous. I can't help but think that this roller coaster of reality is reflected in the body of work you hold in your hands.

Some of you will like it. Some of you will love it. Some of you might hate it. But I knew that when I accepted the challenge. I like to shake things up a bit. After all, I'm on Team Frankenstein, remember?

Be Grim,

MARY WOLLSTONECRAFT SHELLEY was born on August 30, 1797, into a life of personal tragedy. In 1816, she married the poet Percy Bysshe Shelley, and that summer traveled with him and a host of other Romantic intellectuals to Geneva. Her greatest achievement was piecing together one of the most terrifying and renowned stories of all time: *Frankenstein; or, The Modern Prometheus.* Shelley conceived *Frankenstein* in, according to her, "a waking dream." This vision was simply of a student kneeling before a corpse brought to life. Yet this tale of a mad creator and his abomination has inspired a multitude of storytellers and artists. She died on February 1, 1851.

GRIS GRIMLY was born much later, but he too experienced tragedy and dismay throughout his life. Considered a Mad Creator among colleagues, he is known for collecting raw materials and assembling them into his own wretched creations. These reanimated tales include *Edgar Allan Poe's Tales of Mystery and Madness, Edgar Allan Poe's Tales of Death and Dementia, The Legend of Sleepy Hollow*, and *Pinocchio.* He has also given life to original forms like Neil Gaiman's *The Dangerous Alphabet* and his own Wicked Nursery Rhymes series, among other demented favorites.

www.madcreator.com